BEST BOOKS 倍斯特出版事業有限公司
Best Publishing Ltd.

Speaking and E-mail for
International Trade and Business

國貿人 口說 E-mail

在全世界做生意

必備關鍵

U0066435

知道如何議價嗎？產品缺貨怎麼辦？○○○○問題要怎麼說？

3大學習關鍵從容應對各種國貿疑難！

陳幸美 ◎ 著

看「情境對話」，打通你說國貿專業英語任督二脈！
從情境對話學習國貿人必會的口語語彙和句型，在各流程上應
對自如，處理起零件延誤等高階難題也講出一口嚇嚇叫英語！

學「王牌助理的小祕訣」
成為主管的萬能幫手、客戶眼中的貼心王！
由王牌助理小秘訣掌握各職場眉角，同樣是負責相同的國
貿交辦事項，你卻總能設想更周到，在主管和客戶心中印
象滿分，於起跑點就遙遙領先其他同儕。

讀「E-mail」信件，下筆時擺脫
「腦筋空白」、「看螢幕發呆」的窘境！
從E-mail中熟悉各句型使用，在分批出貨、下單後追
加數量、向廠商催款等信件中，用最清楚的表達、最
道地的用語寫出廠商都能輕易讀懂的信件。

Author's
作者序 Preface

　　無論你是國貿或商業相關科系畢業的同學們，或是外語相關科系畢業或是有留學背景的同學們。其實大家都是從實際的國貿工作所遇到的狀況中才發現自己不足的部分。《國貿人邁向國際的必備關鍵英語口說＋E-mail》涵蓋了實際當英文祕書會遇到的大小狀況，不但可以補強國貿知識更可以增強用英語回答問題的技巧，讓你臨危不亂。

　　當個王牌助理／英文秘書除了要細心地了解公司的業務和運作流程之外，更重要的是如何可以把老闆的意思明確地傳達給客戶，作為溝通的橋樑。當你能夠比老闆更早看出合約上有錯誤或是不合理的地方，那你就不再只是個單純的助理，你就是一個準備好升職，可以獨當一面的員工了。希望讀者們都能順利地善用語言優勢來展現實力。

陳幸美

Editor's
編者序 Preface

《國貿人邁向國際的必備關鍵英語口說＋**E-mail**》分別在口說跟寫作上介紹了 36 個常見主題，在口說中提供了即效性的應答，語言使用簡潔且道地，汰除了教科書中生硬、英語使用者聽不懂或理解上有困難的對話應答。讀者能輕易與職場接軌、立即上手，以英語輕鬆向其他公司詢價、報價、了解規格、處理貨物運送問題以及與外籍工程師應對。

在寫作中，除了介紹常見的國貿主題外，與考用書籍及 E-mail 書作出了區隔，使讀者能以最清晰的語言表達提升工作效能，無形中省去後續在電話、信件或開會上，需要重新確認事情所需要花費的時間。最後，很感謝陳幸美老師，在撰寫中花費許多心思，呈現出這本即效性跟實用性極強的國貿書籍。

編輯部敬上

CONTENTS

目錄

PART 02 國貿寫作篇

在台灣的英語教學模式下，我們較少開口講英語，也使得大家常覺得有口難開？聽到別人講得頭頭是道，但換做自己時卻有口難開。

這個情況在平常還好，但步入職場後卻是種無形的壓力，尤其是剛入行時儘管拿著新多益高分，卻常發現自己不知道在詢價、報價、規格、下單、出貨等主題，該用甚麼語句來表達才比較好呢？如果你也有這樣的困擾，趕快一起來看看國貿口說篇的介紹吧！

Unit 1
詢問對方聯絡人資料

前情提要

　　英文秘書在網路上找到這家國外公司可能可以供應公司需要的產品，她想在拜訪前，先發封郵件詢問聯絡人的資料。

人物角色

- Joyce　　　　　英文秘書
- Mark　　　　　對方公司總機

情境對話　🎧 MP3 01

Joyce: Hello, this is Joyce Lin calling from Sevenseas company from Taiwan. We are currently **looking for** new suppliers for a wide range of seafood, and I would like to send an enquiry to your Sales Department, would you be able to tell me who should I **address to**?

喬伊斯：您好，我是台灣七海公司的喬伊斯‧林，我們目前在尋找能提供各式各樣海鮮的供應商，我想要寄份詢價單過去貴公司的銷售部門，請問跟誰聯繫呢？

Mark: It would be Erik Theroux; it's Erik with a "K". He is our regional sales manager for Asia.

馬克：請你發給艾瑞克瑟魯，艾瑞克的拼法字尾是「K」喔！他是我們亞太區的銷售經理。

Joyce: Thanks for that. Would you be able to spell his last name for me please?

喬伊斯：謝謝，那請問瑟魯怎麼拼呢？

Mark: It is T, H, E, R, O, U, X. Would you like me to **put you through**? He is in **at the moment**.

馬克：是 T, H, E, R, O, U, X. 需要幫你轉接嗎？他現在有空。

Joyce: Thanks, that would be great.

喬伊斯：好的，麻煩你。

慣用語

1. **look for** 尋找

The price went up 20% since the beginning of the year. I think I will start to **look for** a new supplier.

從年初開始價格已經漲了兩成。我覺得是時候要開發新的供應商了。

---

2. **address to** 寫給某人

This letter is **addressed to** the Finance Department. Just pass it to Linda.

這封信是寄給財務部的，交給琳達就可以。

---

3. **put someone through** 幫某人把電話轉接過去

Can you **put me through** to Mr. Smith, please?

麻煩請你幫我轉接史密斯先生。

---

4. **at the moment** 目前，現在

He is away for business **at the moment**. Can I take a message for him?

他去出差了，目前不在，您需要留言嗎？

王牌助理的小祕訣

　　在對話裡常常會聽到沒聽過的名字，如果沒聽清楚的話，不妨禮貌地請對方拼出姓名的正確拼法與發音，然後建檔存底。因為如果在郵件或是傳真上拼錯別人的名字，有些外國人可是會很介意的。假設對方的名字是一般的拼法（如：Eric），通常外國人他會假設你了解，不會特別強調。但因為歐美國家的國情及語系不同，一樣的英文名字可以有各式各樣的拼法。

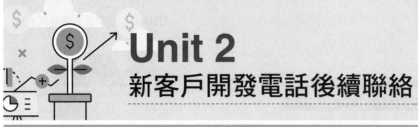

Unit 2
新客戶開發電話後續聯絡

前情提要

公司的英文秘書發了公司簡介過去給新供應商，她想確認對方是否有收到。

人物角色

- Joyce　　　　　英文／國貿秘書
- Mr. Theroux　　新供應商

情境對話　🎧 MP3 02

Joyce: Hello, Mr. Theroux, this is Joyce Lin calling from Sevenseas company in Taiwan. I was wondering whether you have received the email I sent a few days ago?

Mr. Theroux: Oh yes, I can recall. Just let me **pull out** the email since I **got you on the phone**.

喬伊斯： 瑟魯先生您好，我是台灣七海公司的喬伊斯・林，我想請問你有收到我發給您的郵件嗎？

瑟魯先生： 喔，有的，我記得。請等一下既然你在線上，讓我把郵件調出來。

14

Joyce: Certainly.

喬伊斯：好的，沒問題。

Mr. Theroux: In your email you mentioned that you are looking for salmon and lobsters; however, we don't **deal with** those items but I can definitely **help you out** with prawns. We get steady supplies of tiger prawns. Are you looking for live ones or frozen ones?

瑟魯先生：你的信件裡面提到説你們再找鮭魚還有龍蝦，這個我幫不上忙，可是蝦子的話我是能幫到忙。我們有固定配合的廠商供應草蝦，請問你們要的是活的還是冷凍的？

Joyce: We are looking for the cooked frozen prawns.

喬伊斯：我們要的是熟凍的蝦子。

Mr. Theroux: That's great, I will organize a quotation for you right away.

瑟魯先生：那好，我馬上幫你們報價。

 慣用語

1. **pull out** 調出來

I have to **pull out** all the sales records from last month to do the sales report.

我要把上個月的銷售紀錄都調出來才可以做銷售報告。

---

2. **got someone on the phone** 剛好某人打電話來

While you **got him on the phone**, can you check with him whether there are more orders from today?

趁他還在線上,你趕快跟他確認看今天早上的訂單是否都給我了嗎?

---

3. **deal with** 處理,經手

I have to check with the accountant for you. I don't **deal with** finance.

我幫你問一下會計,因為錢的事不是我負責的。

---

4. **help someone out** 幫助,幫上某人忙

Sarah got visitors with her today, so I will be **helping her out** to mind the front desk.

莎拉今天要接待訪客,所以櫃檯的事就由我幫忙。

王牌助理的小祕訣

　　客戶開發信有點像亂槍打鳥，所以事後的電話確認很重要，電話中可以立即釐清很多郵件裡沒有交代清楚的細節，例如進口海鮮除了分成活海鮮跟冷凍海鮮之外，冷凍海鮮還分為生的或是煮熟的。各個行業要求的細節不同，很難在客戶開發信裡面解釋清楚，尤其是可以客製化的商品，或是沒有替代性的商品，在詢價的階段如果可以確認清楚，後續可以省下很多郵件上往返的時間。

前情提要

秘書趁著跟新供應商講電話的機會，順便多了解一下是否有其他的合作機會。

人物角色

- Joyce　　　　　英文／國貿秘書
- Mr. Theroux　　新供應商

情境對話　 MP3 03

Joyce: What other items can you supply?

Mr. Theroux: Well, **other than** tiger prawns, we also process a lot of squids. Our squid rings are very popular in the US. We have a factory that we **work with.** I know there is a big market for squid tentacles in Asia, would it be

喬伊斯：請問你們還可以提供那些產品？

瑟魯先生：嗯，除了草蝦之外，我們還有處理很多魷魚，我們的魷魚圈在美國市場很受歡迎，我們有專門的加工廠跟我們配合。我知道魷魚鬚在

something you are **looking for**?

Joyce: Hmmm.. I am not sure at this stage, our clients have never **asked for** squid tentacles, and it doesn't mean we don't have a market for it. I could do a little survey among our customers and see if they are interested. Can you give me more information please?

Mr. Theroux: They are cleaned and frozen in vacuum sealed bags. Each bag is two kilos.

亞洲市場用量很多，你們會有興趣嗎？

喬伊斯： 這個嘛，現階段我不太確定，我們的客戶沒有跟我們提過他們有這方面的需求，而且這不代表我們沒有市場。我可以做些調查，問一下我們的客戶們，看他們有沒有意願，你可以跟我介紹一下大概的包裝方式嗎？

瑟魯先生： 都清理過而且真空包裝的冷凍魷魚鬚，每包兩公斤裝。

 慣用語

1. **other than** 除了

What else did you do **other than** staying at home on the weekend?

你周末除了待在家之外還做了什麼？

---

2. **work with** 配合、合作

We have a specific courier company that we **work with**. They always give us a good deal.

我們有固定配合的貨運公司，他們都會算我們便宜。

---

3. **There is a market for something** 對於某物有需求、有這個市場

I believe **there is a market for** luxury cars in China based on the finding of this report.

看過這份報告之後，我相信中國對高級車款會有需求。

---

4. **ask for** 詢問

I will be away for business in the next two weeks, please **ask for** Henry if you need assistance.

我未來兩周都會去出差，有什麼事麻煩找亨利幫忙。

王牌助理的小祕訣

　　既然有心打電話過去新的國外供應商，就應該趁這個機會多了解一下對方的公司，因為搞不好除了原來談的案子，未來可能還會有其他合作的機會。積極一點的供應商也會藉這個機會推銷或是介紹他們公司的其他產品或專門的領域。在與新公司接洽的初期，一通電話可以迅速釐清未來合作機會的可能性，如果確認沒機會合作，就可以尋找下一個合適的供應商或是客戶。

Unit 4
報價同等品

 **前情提要**

Jamie 跟國外廠商詢價一個機械零件，後來廠商通知停產了。

 人物角色

- Linda　　　　　國外供應商
- Jamie　　　　　英文／國貿秘書

情境對話 🎧 MP3 04

Linda: Hey Jamie, I have a bad news for you, the part that you enquired yesterday is discontinued, and they do have a replacement, but the maker would need your machine type and serial number to determine whether the new part would suit your machine.

琳達：嗨！傑米，我有個壞的消息要跟你說，你昨天詢價的那個組件已經停產了，原廠是有替代品，可是你需要提供機台號碼還有型號製造商才能確認替代品能不能用在你的機台上。

Jamie: Right, thanks for letting me know, but I don't **have the information handy**. I need to **check with** the end user and ask them to provide the information. I might have to **get back to** you on Monday or even on Tuesday.

Linda: No pressure! Just **call me back** whenever you got the detail.

傑米：好的，謝謝你跟我說，我手邊目前沒有這些資訊，我需要跟客戶確認。可能要下星期一或甚至到星期二才能回覆給你。

琳達：沒問題，有資料再打給我就好。

01 PART 國貿口說篇

02 PART 國貿寫作篇

慣用語

1. have something handy 把某物準備好

Make sure you **have all the client contact detail handy.** You would need to for emergency.

記得要把客戶的聯絡資料準備好，有急事的時候會用得上。

2. check with someone 詢問某人的意見

I need to **check with** Tony to see if he can attend the meeting on my behalf.

我需要問一下東尼看他是不是可以代表我去開會。

3. get back to someone 回覆給某人

Don't forget to **get back to** Jessica. She is still waiting for an answer.

別忘了潔西卡還在等你的回覆。

4. call someone back 回電話給某人

I just remembered that I forgot to **call her back.**

我剛剛才想起來我忘了回她電話。

 **王牌助理的小祕訣**

　　詢價單的明細常常會需要再確認，尤其是牽涉到機械或設計上的需求，商品必須要很精準地達到客戶的要求。貿易公司畢竟不是使用者本身，所以一些比較詳細的歷史規格明細公司也不會有資料，所以一定要跟客戶求證，千萬不要亂猜測。供應商也了解這種情況，所以無法及時回覆是可以接受的情況，只要先跟供應商打個招呼，大家有共識就可以了。

Unit 5
規格不清楚

 **前情提要**

Rosie 發了張詢價單過去給廠商，廠商有點疑問打電話過來問清楚。

人物角色

• Tom　　　　　國外供應商
• Rosie　　　　英文／國貿秘書

情境對話 🎧 MP3 05

Tom: Hi Rosie, thanks for the enquiry, but it seems a bit confusing. Can I just **go through** the details again with you please?

湯姆：蘿西您好，謝謝你的詢價單，可是明細有點不清楚，我想跟你再確認一下好嗎？

Rosie: Of course, what seems to be the problem?

蘿西：沒問題，是哪裡不清楚呢？

Tom: The part number that you provided doesn't seem like our standard part number and I **double checked** our database, it is not our part.

Rosie: Right, can you tell me what your standard part number looks like?

Tom: Sure, for pumps, it normally started with PS34. The number you provided is KS8A, I think **it could have been** PS34, but you'd better check again with the end user **just to be on the safe side**.

湯姆：你提供的型號不太像我們公司的標準型號，我也重新確認過公司的系統，我們沒有這個型號。

蘿西：這樣啊，那你可以跟我說你們公司的型號大概是怎麼樣？

湯姆：可以，如果是幫浦的話，通常是PS34 開頭的，你給我的型號是KS8A，我猜有可能是 PS34，可是你最好跟客戶再確認一下。

慣用語

1. go through 對照、再檢查一次

Can we **go through** the speech again, please? I am worried that I would make mistakes.

我們可以再對照一次講稿的內容嗎？我怕我會出錯。

---

2. double check 再次確認

I am not sure about our refund policy; you might want to **double check** with the manager.

我不太清楚我們的退貨條件，你可能要再跟經理確認一下。

---

3. it could have been 有可能是

Well, I think **it could have been** her, but I am just not sure.

嗯，我覺得有可能是她，可是我真的不確定。

---

4. just to be on the safe side 這樣比較保險

Maybe we should schedule extra staffs for the weekend rush **just to be on the safe side**.

我們不如多安排一點人手來應付周末的人潮，這樣比較保險。

王牌助理的小祕訣

　　因為詢價的商品資訊大部分都是由客戶提供的，如果這個商品客戶以前沒有跟公司購買過，公司也不會知道明細是否有錯誤，所以這種情況下就一定要找客戶再確認一次，或是可以請客戶提供照片，或是原始產品型錄的資訊。同樣的，如果覺得國外報價單上有不清楚的地方，一定要再次澄清，不然訂錯商品後續要更換或退款都很麻煩。

Unit 6
修改規格請重報

前情提要

　　Gina 請國外廠商報價零件,但是客戶想把整組換掉,她打電話去請廠商重新報價。

人物角色

- Gina　　　　英文／國貿秘書
- Kevin　　　　國外供應商

情境對話

Gina: Hello, Kevin. How's going? You know the enquiry I sent you **the other day** for two knife rollers?

吉娜:凱文您好,你記得我前幾天傳給你的詢價單嗎?就是詢價兩個滾刀那張。

Kevin: Yes, I can recall.

凱文:有,我記得。

Gina: I just **got off the phone with** the client, and they are thinking about replacing the complete

吉娜:客戶剛打來說他們想乾脆把整組的裁切設備更新,升級

cutting unit and **upgrading to** the new automatic system. Is it possible for you to send us another quotation for a completed cutting unit with one spare roller please? Don't worry about those two rollers.

Kevin: Ok, but I have to check whether the new cutting unit can be installed onto your client's machine first. I know some of them are not **compatible with** the original machine.

成最新型的自動系統。你可以幫我報價一組新的裁切設備加上一個備品滾刀？那兩組滾刀就不用報了。

凱文： 我知道了，可是我要先查一下新的裁切設備是不是可以裝在你們客戶的機台上，因為有些舊的機型沒有辦法修改。

01
PART
國貿口說篇

02
PART
國貿寫作篇

 **慣用語**

1. **the other day 前幾天**

I saw that woman **the other day** when I was out shopping.

前幾天我在買東西的時候我見過這個女人。

---

2. **got off the phone with someone 跟某人講完電話**

I just **got off the phone with** my boss. He wants me to follow up with the textile case.

我剛跟我老闆講完電話，他交代我要追蹤一下紡織廠的那個案子。

---

3. **upgrade to 升級、更換**

I want to **upgrade** my car **to** an automatic.

我想把我的車換成自排的。

---

4. **compatible with 可相容的、可以配合使用**

The iphone headphone is not **compatible with** Android system.

Iphone 的耳機與安卓系統不相容。

王牌助理的小祕訣

　　客戶三心兩意是常見的事，只是對英文／國貿祕書來說就是要多花一些時間重新跟供應商溝通。因為早先已經傳過詢價單了，相信供應商已經在處理中。如果對方還沒報價，那電話連絡會比較禮貌，這樣也不會浪費供應商的時間與精力。如果對方已經報價了，那更要口頭打聲招呼，因為有些比較積極的供應商在報價後會後續追蹤案子的發展，為什麼報價了卻沒有訂單。

Unit 7
交期太長向廠商詢問原因

Michael 的公司之前向 Zoe 的公司買過一項商品，現在又要再次回購，可是他發現交期比上次長了很多，他致電向 Zoe 詢問。

人物角色

• Michael   客戶
• Zoe   供應商

Michael: Hi Zoe, thanks for your quotation. I did notice something unusual, and I thought **I'd better** check with you again.

麥可：柔伊你好，謝謝你的報價，報價單有點不尋常，我想我最好再跟你確認一次。

Zoe: Of course. You are referring to the quotation I sent yesterday if I am not wrong?

柔伊：當然，如果我沒想錯的話，你是指我昨天傳的那張嗎？

Michael: Yeah, **that's it.**

麥可：是的，沒錯。

Zoe: Ok, what is wrong with it?

柔伊：嗯，是哪裡有問題呢？

Michael: You know we ordered the same thing last year, but the delivery was only 4 weeks. Is there any reason why the delivery has been pushed back to 8 weeks?

麥可：你知道我們去年有買過同樣的產品，可是那時候交期只有四個星期，為什麼現在變成八星期呢？

Zoe: Right, **the thing is**, there is **a bit of delay** on the raw material. We are also waiting for it to arrive before we can start to manufacture.

柔伊：嗯，事情是因為目前原材料的交期有點延誤，我們也還在等東西來才可以開始加工。

 **慣用語**

1. someone had better 某人…最好…

You'd better finish this report before lunch time. I think Jim needs it for the meeting at 3.

你最好在中午前把這份報告打好,吉姆三點開會的時候可能要用到。

---

2. that's it 答對了,就是這樣

That's it! I finally figured it out.

就是這樣了。我終於想出來了!

---

3. the thing is… 可是,是這樣的…

The thing is, I don't want to tell him because I don't know how he feels about me.

是這樣的,因為我不知道他是怎麼看待我的,所以我不想跟他提。

---

4. a bit of delay 延遲,出狀況

I am afraid you won't be able to pick up your car today. There is **a bit of delay,** and the car is not ready.

很抱歉你今天可能沒有辦法把車牽回去,因為有點狀況,你的車還沒弄好。

王牌助理的小祕訣

　　對於有前購經驗的商品，通常公司還是會再次跟供應商確認再報價給客戶，以避免漲價或是存貨不足而耽誤到交貨的情況發生。如果真的遇到漲價或交期延長的情況，客戶一定會提出疑問，所以不如主動先與國外詢問一下，才不會在客戶問到的時候答不出來。在本身準備比較充足的情況下也會讓公司顯得比較專業，上司也會覺得你有獨當一面的能力。

01
PART
國貿口說篇

02
PART
國貿寫作篇

Unit 8
替代品再次確認

前情提要

Sandra 向 Thomas 的公司詢價一個零件，可是報價單上的型號卻跟他詢價的內容不同，他致電向 Sandra 確認。

人物角色

- Sandra　　　　買家
- Thomas　　　　賣家

情境對話 MP3 08

Sandra: Hello Thomas. Thanks you for your quotation. I noticed the part number is not what we enquired for, and it was not specified on the quotation. Is this a replacement?

珊卓：湯瑪士您好，謝謝你的報價單，可是我發現你報的型號跟我們詢價的不一樣，而且報價單上沒有特別註明，這是替代品嗎？

Thomas: It is actually an equivalent from a different maker,

湯瑪士：那其實是不同製造商生產的同等

but the specification is **the same as** the part that you enquired for. It is 30% **cheaper than** the original Honeywell one.

Sandra: Well, luckily **double-checked with** you before I send the quotation to the client. Can you send me another quotation for the original part, please? I will mention to the end user about the price difference to see if they are **willing to** switch to the equivalent.

品,規格跟你詢價的商品是一樣的,可是價格比原廠漢威公司的便宜了三成。

珊卓:嗯,還好我在報價給客戶之前有跟你再次查證,你可以報價一個原廠的產品給我嗎?我會跟使用客戶提一下價格的區別,看看他們是不是願意用同等品。

慣用語

1. the same as something 與某物相同

His phone is **the same as** mine.

他的手機跟我的一樣。

---

2. cheaper than something 比某物便宜

I can't believe petrol is **cheaper than** water in the middle East.

我不敢相信在中東汽油比水便宜。

---

3. double-check with someone 再次澄清

I need to **double-check with** Anna. I am not sure what she wants me to do with her mails.

我需要再問一下安娜，我不確定她的郵件要怎們處理。

---

4. willing to 願意

I am **willing to** increase my offer to 10 dollars.

我願意把金額加到十塊錢。

王牌助理的小祕訣

　　廠商傳來的報價單一定要仔細按對，因為很多時候報價的人並沒有仔細看清楚詢價的內容，如果覺得有疑慮，一定要跟廠商再次確認。很多時候再次確認時就會發現廠商報的並不是我們詢價的產品。最糟的情況是沒有確認就報給客戶，客戶也下訂單了，但是到貨時才發現商品並不是客戶要的。這時公司不但可能損失運費，貨物可能也無法退換，客戶那裡更難交代。

Unit 9
下單後要追加數量

前情提要

　　Claire 的公司向 John 的公司訂了 500 包的黏著劑，John 報價的時候有提到如果訂 1000 包的話則享有數量折扣。Claire 在跟客戶家戶接洽過後決定多訂 500 包。

人物角色

- Claire　　　　買家
- John　　　　賣家

情境對話　　MP3 09

Claire: Hey John, you know that purchase order I sent two days ago for 500 packets of glue. Is it too late to change it to 1000 packets?

克萊兒：你好約翰，你知道我兩天前傳過去的那張 500 包黏著劑的那張訂單，我可以改成訂 1000 包嗎？

John: Right, I was just **working on** the order confirmation for you. You

約翰：喔！這樣啊！我剛剛才在處理你的

can change it to 1000 packets if you want.

Claire: Thanks, but I just want to double check whether the delivery remains the same as 2 weeks. We would like to **consolidate into** one shipment to save the shipping cost.

John: Let me check our inventory list. Well, I can ship all 1000 packets for you in 3 weeks, would it be ok?

Claire: That would be great. **In that case** are we **entitled to** the quantity discount?

John: Of course you are.

訂單確認書，要改成 1000 包的話，沒有問題啊。

克萊兒：好的，謝謝，可是我想再跟你確認一次這樣的話交期還是維持兩個星期嗎？我們想要跟之前的 500 包併貨一起出，這樣可以省一筆運費。

約翰：讓我看一下我們的庫存表，這樣的話我們最快要三個星期的時間才能幫你出貨總計 1000 包的量，這樣可以接受嗎？

克萊兒：這樣沒問題，如果是這樣的話，那你們是不是會給我數量折扣？

約翰：當然可以。

01 PART 國貿口說篇

02 PART 國貿寫作篇

慣用語

1. work on something 處理中、正在安排

I have been **working on** this project since 3 months ago.

我三個月前開始負責這個專案。

----

2. consolidate into 集中、合併

I got three orders ready for Amanda. I will **consolidate into** a single shipment for her.

我有三個亞曼達的訂單都好了，我會幫她併貨一起出。

----

3. in that case 這樣的話

In that case, I think I will go in to work early tomorrow morning.

如果是這樣的話，那我明天一早一點到公司好了。

----

4. be entitled to 有資格

You are **entitled to** annual bonus once you stayed a full year in this company.

如果你在公司待滿一年後，你有就資格可以領年終。

王牌助理的小祕訣

　　如果是需求量大的消耗品，常常賣家會提供數量折扣，買越多越划算。可是因為不是每間公司都有倉儲的場地，所以就算知道價格比較便宜，卻不見得每個客戶都會想搶便宜。可是如果下了訂單之後要追加數量話，照理說是可以享有折扣的。除了享有數量折扣外，有的賣家願意幫買家分批出貨，這樣買家就沒有倉儲的麻煩。可是有些賣家堅持一次要把貨出足才有折扣。

Unit 10
下單後發現錯誤

Jenny 在傳訂單給 Jimmy 的公司之後，突然發現訂單上的明細好像有問題，他馬上打電話過去請 Jimmy 先暫停處理這張訂單。

人物角色

• Jenny
• Jimmy

情境對話 MP3 10

Jenny: Hello Jimmy, I have an emergency I hope you can help me. Can you **put** the purchase order that I sent last week **on hold for the time being**? I just realized the voltage might not be correct, and I have to check with the end user again.

珍妮：阿蘭娜你好，我有件急事需要你的幫忙，你可不可以把我上星期傳過去的訂單先暫停處理？我剛剛發現電壓好像不對，可是我必須再跟客戶確認一次。

Jimmy: Right, I would have to contact the manufacturer and see whether that is possible. I can't guarantee anything at this stage, but I will **try my best**. When do you think you can get back to me about the correct voltage?

Jenny: I will do it **first thing tomorrow** for sure. Thanks for trying. I hope I am not in too much trouble.

阿蘭娜：這樣啊，我可能要先問一下製造商看是不是可以先暫停，可是我不能保證一定可以。你什麼時候可以跟我確定電壓的規格？

珍妮：我明天早上會優先處理，謝謝你的好意，希望我沒有闖大禍。

 **慣用語**

1. put something / someone on hold 暫停、稍等

Sorry I can **put you on hold** for a minute, please. I am on another line.

可以麻煩請你稍等嗎？我現在還在接另一通電話。

---

2. for the time being 短暫的、此刻、目前

I think our jobs are safe **for the time being**, but I think the restructure is still coming.

現在這個階段我們的工作還保得住，可是我猜公司重整是遲早的事。

---

3. try someone's best 盡力

I will **try my best** not to let you down.

我會盡力去做不會讓你失望的。

---

4. first thing tomorrow 明早立即處理

I promise the report will be ready for you **first thing tomorrow**.

我保證那份報表明天你進公司就會在你桌上。

王牌助理的小祕訣

在處理公司的事務上，犯錯是無可厚非的事，如果能夠及時處理與補救那倒也還好。最怕的是在收到貨品的時候才發現大錯已鑄成。如果可以在處理詢價的時候就小心行事，下訂單之前再三確認內容，那就可以減少犯錯的機率。通常賣家在收到訂單後會回傳訂單確認書給買家，這應該是抓錯誤的最後機會，在確認回傳之後要修改可能就不容易了。

Unit 11
提醒合約回傳

前情提要

Jeremy 的公司向 Belinda 的公司下了訂單，可是一直還在等 Belinda 傳訂單確認書給她。

人物角色

- Jeremy　　　買方
- Belinda　　　賣方

情境對話  MP3 11

Jeremy: Hello, this is Jeremy calling from Tai-Guang trading company in Taiwan. I was wondering whether you have received our purchase order number PO100165 dated 13th March 2017.

傑瑞米：您好，我是台灣台光貿易公司的崔西，我想請問一下您有沒有收到我們 2017 年 3 月 13 號傳的訂單？訂單號碼是 PO100165？

Belinda: Let me check my files. Was it on 13th March?

柏琳達：讓我看一下我的檔案，你是說三月十三號傳的嗎？

Jeremy: Yes, it was, and we are still **waiting for** your order confirmation.

Belinda: Right, is that what you are **calling about**? Sorry for the delay. I will be **on to it**, and you should have it by this afternoon.

Jeremy: Thanks for that. Can you also attach a copy of your bank detail please? We haven't had it on record.

Belinda: Sure thing.

傑瑞米：是的，沒錯。我們一直還在等妳的訂單確認書。

柏琳達：好的，請問你特別打電話過來是這個原因嗎？很抱歉耽誤到你的時間，我會馬上處理，你應該今天下午就會收到。

傑瑞米：很謝謝你，可以麻煩你順便傳一份你的匯款帳號給我嗎？我們目前還沒有資料可以留底。

柏琳達：沒問題。

01 PART 國貿口說篇

02 PART 國貿寫作篇

 **慣用語**

1. waiting for 等待

I am still **waiting for** the call from Joe to see if I am on duty tomorrow.

我還在等喬回給我,他要跟我確認我明天是不是要值班。

---

2. calling about 打電話來的原因、請某人聽電話

The manager is on the phone. He is **calling about** Jacky.

經理打電話進來,他要找傑克。

---

3. on to it 處理、進行中

I know this invoice needs to be fixed. I am **on to it**.

我知道這份對帳單要重做,我會處理。

---

4. sure thing 當然、一定

Sure thing! I can help you with entertaining the visitors.

當然,我可以幫你招待客戶。

王牌助理的小祕訣

　　大部分的公司在收到訂單之後都會傳一份訂單確認書給買方，尤其是第一次交易的公司。對於第一次交易的公司通常會要求下訂單之後全額付清。有些公司只是把你的訂單上蓋個確認章然後回傳給你，這也視同訂單確認。如果沒有收到訂單確認，最好打個電話確認是否賣方是在處理中。很多時候心理假設對方已在處理中，打了電話才發現原來訂單根本沒收到。

01
PART
國貿口說篇

02
PART
國貿寫作篇

Unit 12
提醒付款條件

　　Jason 收到 Sue 公司的訂單，處理之後一直還在等匯款，她打電話過去提醒一下。

人物角色

- Jason　　　　　　賣方
- Nina　　　　　　　買方公司總機小姐
- Sue Marshal　　　買方訂單負責人

情境對話　 MP3 12

Jason: Hello, this is Jason calling from CK trading company in Taiwan. I am ringing regarding an order we received at the beginning of this month from Sue Marshal. I was wondering whether I can **have a word with** her, please?

傑森：您好，我是台灣 CK 貿易公司的艾利，我有些關於貴公司這個月初訂單的問題要找一下蘇・馬修。

Nina: Unfortunately, she is in a meeting at the moment. Can I **take a message?**

Jason: Sure, I would like to check with her whether she has **put in a request** for the down payment to be processed yet. Your order number is 0900234 dated 12th Jan 2017, and the down payment amount is USD 300. Please note the order will only be processed **upon receipt of payment**.

妮娜：不好意思她目前正在開會，您要留話嗎？

傑森：好的麻煩你，我想跟她確認一下她有沒有跟會計交代要匯錢的事。貴公司的訂單號碼是 0900234，日期是 2017 年的 1 月 12 日。訂金的金額是美金三百塊。麻煩請提醒他訂單要收到訂金之後才會開始處理。

01
PART
國
貿
口
說
篇

02
PART
國
貿
寫
作
篇

慣用語

1. have a word with someone 與某人談一談

I don't know what I have done. The manager wants to **have a word with** me.

我不知道我到底做了什麼。經理説要找我談一談。

---

2. take a message 留言

If anyone call me, can you **take a message** please?

如果有人打電話給我，可以麻煩你幫我留言嗎？

---

3. put in a request 申請，要求

I just realised Tommy **put in a request** to be transferred to Sales.

我剛聽説湯米要申請調到銷售部。

---

4. upon receipt of payment 收到款項之後

Your order will be shipped **upon receipt of payment**.

收到錢之後我們會馬上幫你出貨。

王牌助理的小祕訣

　　做生意是很現實的事，在訂金或是款項沒有收到之前訂單就是在等待處理中的狀態。付款的速度會影響最大的就是出貨的時間。所以如果是急件的話，付款絕對不能拖，否則趕不上交貨期被客戶罰款就得不償失。同樣的，站在賣方的立場，如果買方遲遲不付款，可以打個電話去了解一下。在老闆還沒開始追問訂單處理進度之前，王牌助理需要先掌握情況。

Unit 13
希望對方放寬付款條件

前情提要

　　Chris 打電話過去給國外供應商討論是不是可以修改付款條件。

人物角色

- Chris 　　　　買方
- Miranda 　　　賣方

情境對話　🎧 MP3 13

Chris: Hello Miranda, **if it's not too much to ask**, I am hoping that you can do us a favor.

克里斯：你好瑪琳達，我希望這不會太麻煩你，我有事要拜託你。

Miranda: Okay. What is it?

瑪琳達：好，你說說看。

Chris: Well, the business is a bit slow in the past few months. We

克里斯：是因為這幾個月生意比較不好，

are having a bit of cash flow issues. I was just wondering whether we could **come out with** new payment terms.

我們的現金有點周轉不靈，我是想問妳我們可不可以研商一下是不是可以改一下付款條件。

Miranda: Hmmm, I would have to ask my boss. You know **it is purely his call**. Just curious, what kind of payment terms are you proposing?

瑪琳達：這個嘛，我要跟我老闆商量一下，你知道這種事都是他決定。只是問一下，你是想要怎麼改？

Chris: If you can **put in a good word** for us and extend the payment cycle from 60 days to 90 days, then it would be really helpful.

克里斯：如果你可以幫我們跟老闆求個情，讓他同意把 60 天延長為 90 天那就太好了。

01
PART
國貿口說篇

02
PART
國貿寫作篇

慣用語

1. if it's not too much to ask 如果不是太麻煩的話

If it's not too much to ask, it will be great if you can take over my shift on Saturday.

如果不是太麻煩你的話，星期六可以跟你調班的話那就太棒了！

----

2. come out with something 想出、構想、整理出來

I need to **come out with some fresh ideas** to impress my boss.

我需要想一些比較有新意的構想，這樣才能打動我的老闆。

----

3. it is someone's call 只有某人可以決定

I really want to help you but you know **it is not my call**.

我真的很想幫你，可是這不是我可以決定的。

----

4. put in a few good words 說幾句好話、求情

I want that promotion so bad. Do you think you can **put in a few good words for** me?

我好想要那個職位，你可以幫我美言幾句嗎？

💡 **王牌助理的小祕訣**

　　通常每間公司都有固定的付款條件（Payment terms）例如：新客戶需全額付清，舊客戶就可以月結之類的。有時候在經濟情況比較不好或是買方公司周轉有問題的時候，買方可能會提出延長付款周期的要求。因為這牽涉到賣方公司的財務情況，所以需要知會老闆或是財務部門，讓公司做決定。如果買方要求延長付款週期其實也是一種警訊，賣方公司也需要小心。

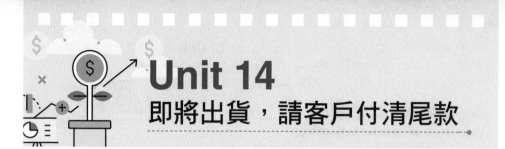

Unit 14
即將出貨，請客戶付清尾款

前情提要

　　Sarah 公司已經準備要出貨了，現在就等 Justin 的公司把尾款付清。

人物角色

- Sarah　　　　賣方
- Justin　　　　買方

情境對話 🎧 MP3 14

Sarah: How are you, Olivia?

莎拉：你好嗎？奧莉維亞？

Justin: I am good, thanks ! What can I do for you?

賈斯丁：我很好，謝謝你，可以幫你什麼忙嗎？

Sarah: Just a **courtesy call** to let you know the shipment is ready for your order number PP88938. The

莎拉：我打來是好意提醒你，你訂單 PP88938 的貨已

initial payment of USD 500 was received December last year and the remaining balance is USD 1500. Would you be able to arrange the payment for us in the next few days **if possible**?

Justin: Sure, not a problem, **just do me a favor**, can you send us a shipping notice for record keeping purposes, and I will **forward it to the accounts** for you.

經好了，我們去年十二月已經收了 500 美金的訂金，尾款還剩 1500 美金，可以麻煩你這幾天內幫我們安排付款嗎？

賈斯丁：當然，沒有問題。可以請你幫我個忙嗎，麻煩你傳一張簡短的出貨通知給我做紀錄嗎？我會交代給會計部門。

慣用語

1. courtesy call 好意的電話提醒

I got a **courtesy call** from my credit card company to say they haven't received the payment.

我接到信用卡公司打來的電話説我尚未付款。

---

2. if possible 可以的話

Can I have the blue one **if possible**, I really like it.

我可以要那個藍色的嗎？我真的很喜歡。

---

3. do me a favor 幫我個忙、拜託你

Just **do me a favor**, turn the volume down please. I found it very loud.

拜託你把聲音關小一點好不好，我覺得很吵。

---

4. forward something to someone 把某物交給某人

I got these documents for Jonny. Can you **forward them to him**, please?

這些文件是要給強尼的，麻煩你轉交給他。

王牌助理的小祕訣

　　如果有牽涉到訂金與尾款的事，通常在貨物即將出貨前買方需要將尾款付清。下訂單的人只是對方公司聯絡的窗口，通常付款的事都是需要透過會計部門處理。只要將需要的文件，例如出貨通知書（*Shopping notice*）及匯款帳號，或是電話口頭通知，買方公司就會照程序處理。等匯完款項之後再將匯款水單（*Remittance advice*）傳一份給賣方，這樣方便賣方跟他指定的銀行追蹤款項。

Unit 15
匯款單／會計部門

前情提要

　　Justin 已經將款項匯給 Sarah 的公司，她向他確認是否有收到。

人物角色

- Justin　　　　買方
- Sarah　　　　賣方

情境對話　 MP3 15

Justin: Hello Sarah, I am calling to let you know the payment has been made on Monday, and you should have it **by now**.

賈斯丁：你好莎拉，我是打來通知你，尾款已經在星期一匯過去了，你應該已經收到了吧？

Sarah: Oh, **thanks for that**. Would you be able to send me the remittance advice, so we can track the payment with our bank, please?

莎拉：喔！謝謝你幫我處理，你可以把匯款水單傳給我嗎？這樣我可以跟銀行追蹤款項。

Justin: Not a problem. Just let you know we did instruct the bank to cover the bank charge as well. You should receive the exact amount of USD1500.

Sarah: That's great! The Accounting Department will be impressed. The shipment is **ready to go**. I will contact the courier, and the shipment will be **on its way** to you this afternoon.

賈斯丁：沒問題,順便跟你説我有交代銀行手續費的部份我們會負責,你會收到整數 1500 美金。

莎拉：太好了,我們會計會很高興。貨已經好了,我會叫快遞來收貨,下午就會出貨給你。

01
PART
國貿口說篇

02
PART
國貿寫作篇

慣用語

1. **by now** 應該、已經

Are you still working on the report? I thought you would have been done **by now.**

你還在做那份報告嗎？我以為你老早就做完了！

---

2. **thanks for something** 因為某事而感謝

Thanks for the test report, the end user would be pleased.

謝謝你的測試報告，使用客戶這樣就滿意了。

---

3. **ready to go** 準備好了

The projector is **ready to go**. We can have the meeting anytime.

投影機弄好了，隨時可以開會。

---

4. **on someone's way** 在路上了、出發了

Can you tell Richie I am **on my way now**, won't be long.

麻煩你跟瑞奇講一聲我在路上了，馬上到。

王牌助理的小祕訣

　　在匯款之後通知賣方可以加速出貨的速度。有時候國外匯款需要等好幾天才會入帳，在這個情況下有的公司在收到匯款水單之後就會先幫買方出貨，以節省時間。畢竟銀行的匯款水單有公信力，不太可能有問題。入帳時會有手續費的問題，可以直接交代客戶需要負擔手續費，尤其是金額小的交易，因為如果再由賣方負擔手續費，那可能就會虧本。

Unit 16
更改運送方式

前情提要

Pheony 的公司跟 Johnny 的公司下了訂單，Johnny 的報價單有另外報運費跟訂單處理費。Pheony 下訂單後發現其實用公司簽約的快遞運送的話金額差不多，他決定打電話過去問問看可不可以修改。

人物角色

- Pheony   買方
- Johnny   賣方

情境對話  MP3 16

Pheony: Hi Johnny, I need to **make an amendment** regarding the shipping method for our PO number 9900384. I'll just quickly run through it with you before I send the new shipping details to you.

費昂妮：強尼您好，我需要更改訂單號碼 9900384 的運送方式，我先口頭跟你解釋一下再把新運送方式的資料傳給你。

Johnny: Sure, **go ahead**.

強尼：好的，請說。

Pheony: We were going to use your contracted forwarder, but we decided to go with our courier instead since it **works out** about the same but much faster.

Johnny: Sure, we can do that, but you know you **are still liable for** the handling charge.

Pheony: Yes, I do.

Johnny: Ok then, I will revise the order confirmation once I got the courier details from you.

費昂妮：我們本來是要用你們簽約的運送公司，可是我們現在決定要用我們自己的快遞公司去收貨，算起來費用差不多但是比較快。

強尼：當然，我們可以處理，可是要提醒你，這樣的話你還是要付訂單處理費。

費昂妮：嗯，我知道。

強尼：好，那等你傳資料過來之後，我在幫你改訂單確認書。

慣用語

1. make an amendment 做修改

You'd better **make an amendment** on the invitation. You spelled Gary's last name wrong.

你最好把邀請函改一下，你把蓋瑞的姓拼錯了

---

2. go ahead 繼續、確認

I thought about it last night. I decided to **go ahead** with it.

我昨晚考慮了很久，我還是決定要做。

---

3. work out 算出來、搞清楚

If we share a room together, it **works out** about $60 dollars per person.

我算過了，如果我們只訂一間房間，那就是一個人 60 塊。

---

4. be liable for 必須負擔

You **are liable for** all the damages, if you don't have any insurance.

如果你沒有保險的話，出意外的時候你要負擔全部的賠償責任。

王牌助理的小祕訣

　　通常訂單發過去之後，唯一可以修改而且不具爭議性的部分大概就是運送方式了，因為運費是完全與商品的報價分開的。所以雖然賣方的報價有含運費，但是建議運費的部分可以貨比三家，畢竟每間貨運公司或是快遞的強項不同，有的專做歐洲線，有的專做美國線。如果有修改運送方式，建議出貨前再跟賣方提醒，避免賣方把貨送給錯的貨運公司。

Unit 17
有急用請廠商分批出貨

前情提要

Mei-Ling 的公司向 Harrison 的公司訂了十個汽缸，可是客戶突然機台壞掉，急需一個現貨，客戶請 Mei-Ling 跟國外供應商詢問是否可以分批出貨。

人物角色

- Mei-Ling　　　　買方
- Harrison　　　　賣方

情境對話 MP3 17

Mei-Ling: Hello Harrison. I was wondering whether you could help me out. I need to check the progress of one of our orders.

美玲：哈里森您好，你能不能夠幫我一個忙，我想詢問一下我們其中一個訂單的進度。

Harrison: Of course, which order are you **referring to**?

哈里森：沒問題，你說的是哪一個訂單？

Mei-Ling: The PO number is KK12-330. It was for 10 cylinders.

美玲：我們的訂單號碼是 KK12-330，是十個汽缸。

Harrison: Let me see... Well the order won't be ready for another 3 weeks.

哈里森：我看一下，嗯，這個訂單還有三個星期才能供貨。

Mei-Ling: I know, but we have **a situation** here. One of the production lines is down, and the end user desperately needs one to get their machine **up and running**. Would you be able to check whether you can have any in stock and available for shipping immediately? **The rest** can wait until then.

美玲：我知道，可是我們現在有問題，客戶其中一台的機台壞了，現在使用者急需一個汽缸來替換，你能不能蓋查一下你們有沒有一個現貨可以馬上出貨給我們？其他九個可以等到三個禮拜後再出。

慣用語

1. refer to 意指、參考

Which guy are you **referring to**? The one with white shirt or the one with a cap?

你是説哪一個男的？那個穿白襯衫的還是戴棒球帽的那個？

---

2. a situation 有困難

I got **a situation** here. I couldn't work out which price is right.

我真的麻煩大了，我搞不清楚哪一個價錢才是對的。

---

3. up and running 修好、準備好、可以用

I need to get this fax machine **up and running** ASAP. We are expecting an important document.

我需要叫人盡快把傳真機修好，我們在等一封重要的文件。

---

4. the rest 其他的

Where is **the rest** of the report?

報表怎麼只有這一些，其他的呢？

🔍 王牌助理的小祕訣

　　臨時分批出貨（*Partial shipment*）要求通常只有緊急的情況才會發生，畢竟分批出貨代表買方（大部分會轉嫁給客戶）需要負擔兩次運費。在金額小的訂單裡，有時候運費比實際商品的費用還要高，如果不是情非得已，也不會提出要求。可以請賣方查一下是否有現貨或是有沒有調貨的可能，如果都沒有的話也只能請求賣方盡量縮短交期，畢竟在危機解除之前，客戶會一直打來催貨。

Unit 18
確認運送方式

((🔊)) 前情提要

　　Fred 的公司已經準備要出貨了,才發現在 Emma 訂單上並沒有註明運送方式,他打電話過去確認。

👤 人物角色

• Fred　　　　　賣方
• Emma　　　　買方

 情境對話　🎧 MP3 18

Fred: Hi Emma, just to let you know your order number 835001 is **ready to be picked up**. I just noticed that you haven't specified the shipping method on your PO, do you want us to courier it or send it via a forwarder.

佛萊德:艾瑪您好,我是想通知您貴公司的 835001 號訂單已經可以出貨了,可是我發現你們訂單上並沒有註明要用何種運送方式,您想要用快遞出貨還是要用海運出貨?

Emma: Right, **my apology**. Please **hold on a second**, let me check. Do you **happen to** know the dimensions of the package?

艾瑪：喔，這樣啊，很抱歉我疏忽了。請您稍等一下，我來看看。請問貨品的外包裝的尺寸是多少？

Fred: Yes, it is 120×90×50 cm, and the weight is approximately 25 kilos.

佛萊德：嗯，是 120×90×50 公分，總重大概是 25 公斤。

Emma: In that case, please use our CPS to collect account. Our account number is: XX659922.

艾瑪：這樣的話，麻煩您用我們 CPS 快遞的對方付款帳號來出貨，帳號是：XX659922。

慣用語

1. ready to be picked up 可以出貨了、好了

The consignment will be **ready to be picked up** in two days.

委託貨物再過兩天就可以出貨了。

---

2. my apology 我很抱歉、無法出席

Please send **my apology** to the meeting. I am not able to make it.

麻煩通知他們我沒有辦法去開會。

---

3. hold on a second 請稍等

Hold on a second, I think I am supposed to go to an engagement party that day.

等一下，我想起來我以為那天是要去參加一個訂婚喜宴。

---

4. happen to 碰巧、剛好

I **happened to** run into William on my way to Taipei.

我碰巧在前往台北的路上遇到威廉。

王牌助理的小祕訣

　　有時候在下訂單的時候會把運送方式空下來，以等候通知（*To be advised*）的方式表示。可能是因為要等到貨物生產或是包裝完成之後才能確定重量與材積，到時候再以最划算的運送方式出貨，通常廠商如果發現沒有註明的話，在出貨前也會再次確認。快遞的運費高，但是相對的手續費少。海運的運費低廉，可是相關的手續還有報關費用等等卻不少。可以精算之後再做決定。

Unit 19
收到錯誤的商品，要求更換

Terry 的公司三年前向 Lucy 的公司訂過一組有磁性的輸送帶，現在又要訂一組同款的輸送帶可是廠商卻沒注意把磁鐵製成反方向。

人物角色

• Terry　　　　　買方
• Lucy　　　　　賣方

情境對話 MP3 19

Terry: Hello Lucy, there is a problem here. We received the conveyor belt yesterday, but the design is wrong. The build-in magnet **was supposed to** be on the right side, but it was on the left.

泰瑞：露西您好，我們現在有個問題，輸送帶昨天收到了，可是設計上有錯。裡面內建的磁鐵應該是要在右邊，不是左邊。

Lucy: Right, let me check the order. Did you **point out** which

露西：這樣啊！讓我檢查一下你們的訂

side the magnet **is meant to** be on?

Terry: Yes, we did. This conveyor belt is meant to be the replacement for the one we ordered 3 years ago, and with the magnet on the wrong side, there is no way we can use this.

Lucy: Well, I would have to check with the engineering department and **see what we can do.** Do you mind shipping the conveyor back?

單，你有在訂單上有特別註明嗎？

泰瑞：當然有，我們三年前訂過一樣的輸送帶，而這個新的輸送帶是要來更換舊的這個。所以如果磁鐵方向做錯，我們就沒辦法用這個東西了。

露西：我知道了，我會跟工程部門討論，看能怎麼處理。你介意把東西退回來嗎？

01
PART
國貿口說篇

02
PART
國貿寫作篇

慣用語

1. be supposed to 應該

I **am not supposed to** tell you, but I think you'd better be prepared for the meeting tomorrow with the manager.

我是不應該跟你提，可是明天跟經理的約談，你最好要有心理準備。

2. point out 指出

Can you **point out** which design do you like the most please?

你可以告訴我你最喜歡哪一個款式嗎？

3. be meant to 本來應該

Luke **was meant to** take over this project, but now it is assigned to Jimmy.

那個專案本來是要給路克負責的，可是現在指定要給吉米做。

4. see what someone can do 再看看能怎麼處理

I can't guarantee you that I can help you, but I will **see what I can do**.

我不能保證一定能幫你，可是我會盡量。

王牌助理的小祕訣

　　有時候就算跟同一個供應商重複買同一樣的東西，如果對方沒有小心處理的話，也可能會出錯，尤其是經手人有調動的情況下。退換貨事小，可是延誤交期的罰金和多次往返的寄送費用可能讓所有的利潤都賠光。如果單純是賣方的錯，可以試著向賣方爭取貼補運費，對方或許不願意全額負擔，如果極力爭取，有的賣方可能願意部分負擔，這也不無小補。

Unit 20
運送過程損壞，向國外反應

 前情提要

　　Sam 的公司向 Lyndsay 的公司訂了 10 個溫度計，可是收到貨之後發現其中一個溫度計的玻璃破裂。Sam 向 Lyndsay 的公司要求換貨。

 人物角色

- Sam　　　　　　買家
- Lyndsay　　　　賣家

情境對話　🎧 MP3 20

Sam: Hello, Lyndsay, thanks for the shipment, we received it yesterday. But 1 of the temperature gauges is damaged. The protecting glass is broken, can you replace them?

山姆：琳希您好，謝謝你幫我們出貨，我們昨天收到了，可是其中的一個溫度計有破損，上面的保護鏡破掉了，你可以幫我們更換嗎？

Lyndsay: Just **one out of ten**?

琳希：十個裡面破了

Yes, we can replace them, but we **are not responsible for** the additional shipping cost.

一個嗎？沒問題，我們可以更換，可是額外的運費要你們自付。

Sam: Yes, I understand that.

山姆：好，這個我了解。

Lyndsay: Can you arrange for the broken one to be returned, please?

琳希：可以麻煩你把破的那個寄回來嗎？

Sam: Definitely. Since I got you one the phone, can you check whether you have 1 available for shipping immediately?

山姆：那當然，既然你在線上，我可以順便詢問一下你們是否有一個現貨可以馬上出？

Lyndsay: Unfortunately, we don't have any at the moment, but the next batch will be ready in two days. I can organize for 1 to go out to you **straight away if that helps**.

琳希：不好意思沒有，可是下一批貨兩天後就會好，我可以馬上幫你寄個去如果你要的話。

Sam: That would be great.

山姆：好的，那麻煩你。

 慣用語

1. one out of ten 十個中有一個、十分之一（可用不同數量）

I bought a bag of apples from the supermarket yesterday, but 2 out of 5 are rotten.

我昨天到超市買了一包蘋果，可是五個裡面有兩顆是爛掉的。

----

2. be responsible for 負責

Helen **is responsible for** the inventory.

庫存的事是由海倫負責。

----

3. straight away 立即、馬上

He hung up the phone **straight away** as soon as he heard my voice.

他一聽到我的聲音就掛電話。

----

4. if that helps 如果這樣幫的到你、最多也只能這樣

I can drop you off at the train station **if that helps**.

如果你想要的話，我可以載你到火車站。

王牌助理的小祕訣

　　收到貨物出狀況的時候，無論是外觀上的損壞或是內部的功能有問題，可以從幾個方面下手。如果包裝上有明顯的凹陷或破損，那就需要與快遞公司協商，提供證據來爭取賠償。如果無法舉證是快遞公司運送方式的問題，那就要向賣方爭取。如果是可以修理再出售的東西，賣方應該會無償更換，但是買方需要寄回去換貨。換貨時可以考慮用便宜的運送方式寄回去，畢竟只是退回去，沒有急迫性。

Unit 21
海運航班接不上，無法準時交貨

Linda 的公司有商品賣給 Jimmy 的公司，Linda 的船公司剛剛通知他航班有更改，他趕緊先跟 Kelly 打聲招呼。

人物角色

- Linda   賣家
- Jimmy   買家

情境對話 MP3 21

Linda: Hi Jimmy, I just heard from the forwarder, the shipment was scheduled to arrive in Kaohsiung port on 25th Mar, but there is a delay in Singapore. Looks like the shipping vessel would **hang around** Singapore for extra 3-4 days.

琳達：吉米你好，我聽我的船運公司說貨輪本來是預計三月二十五日抵達高雄港，可是在新加坡有些問題耽誤了，看來可能在新加坡會多耽誤三到四天。

Jimmy: Right! Thanks for letting me know. I think extra 3 or 4 days would not cause any problem, but if it is longer than a week, then we might **be in trouble for** missing the deadline.

吉米：這樣啊！謝謝你通知我，如果只是三、四天那倒是還好，只要不要超過一個星期，因為我們可能會因延誤交期而有麻煩。

Linda: There is nothing we can do other than wait. I will **keep an eye on this case,** and I will **keep you posted** when I know more.

琳達：目前我們只能等，我會特別注意這個案子，有消息我會隨時跟你聯絡。

01
PART
國貿口說篇

02
PART
國貿寫作篇

 慣用語

1. hang around 圍繞，留下來

It is getting late, I don't want to **hang around** much longer.

現在有點晚了，我也差不多要走了。

---

2. be in trouble for something 因為某是被牽連，受害

Danny **is in trouble for** sending the order to the wrong client.

丹尼被罵死了，因為他出錯貨，將貨出給了錯的客戶。

---

3. keep an eye on something 注意某事

You'd better **keep an eye on** your purse when you are in a public area.

在公共場所裡，你最好要小心你的皮包。

---

4. keep someone posted 向某人通報，通知

The manager will be away for a week, and make sure you **keep him posted** with any latest news.

經理這個星期都不在，如果有新發展的話，記得要通知他。

王牌助理的小祕訣

　　收到貨物出狀況的時候，無論是外觀上的損壞或是內部的功能有問題，可以從幾個方面下手。如果包裝上有明顯的凹陷或破損，那就需要與快遞公司協商，提供證據來爭取賠償。如果無法舉證是快遞公司運送方式的問題，那就要向賣方爭取。如果是可以修理再出售的東西，賣方應該會無償更換，但是買方需要寄回去換貨。換貨時可以考慮用便宜的運送方式寄回去，畢竟只是退回去，沒有急迫性。

Unit 22
收到的貨物與出貨單內容不符

前情提要

　　Michelle 公司跟 Justin 的公司訂了一批貨，收到貨時發現跟她訂的貨物有出入。

人物角色

• Michelle　　　　買方
• Justin　　　　　賣方

情境對話　🎧 MP3 22

Michelle: Thanks for the shipment, but I think there is a problem. This is not the right order for us.

蜜雪兒：謝謝你的出貨，可是這批貨有點問題，這跟我們訂的貨不一樣。

Justin: Right, can you explain further, please?

賈斯丁：是嗎？可以說清楚一點嗎？

Michelle: Sure, do you have a copy of the packing list handy?

蜜雪兒：當然，你手邊有我們的出貨單嗎？

Justin: <u>Just a minute</u>, I will **<u>look it up</u>**. **<u>Here it is</u>**.

賈斯丁：稍等，我找一下，找到了。

Michelle: On the packing list it shows that we ordered a complete filter system which is housing plus a filter pad, but what we received is only a filter pad replacement. Can you please check your record and send us the filter housing **<u>ASAP</u>** please?

蜜雪兒：在出貨單上顯示我們訂的是整組的過濾器，就是過濾器再加上濾網，可是實際上貨物裡面只有濾網。你可以查一下你的出貨紀錄然後趕快補一個過濾器給我們嗎？

Justin: Ok, I will check with my coworker and let you know shortly.

賈斯丁：好的，我跟我的同事求證一下再跟你說。

慣用語

1. just a minute 請等一下

Just a minute, I am on another line.

請等一下，我正在跟別人講電話。

---

2. look it up / look up something 找出來、查詢

Can you **look up** his last name for me, please?

可以幫我查一下他到底姓什麼嗎？

---

3. here it is 找到了、就是這個

Here it is, I finally found it.

就是這個，我終於找到了。

---

4. ASAP (As soon as possible) 盡快

I am running late. Can you tell Kelly I will be there **ASAP** please?

我遲到了，你可以跟凱利說我會盡快到。

王牌助理的小祕訣

　　每次收到貨物開箱的時候都會擔心收到的貨是不是會有問題，像情境對話裡的情況，完全需要依賴賣方回去追查是哪個環節出錯，可能需要一點時間。因為是出貨短少，所以買方不妨可以提供貨運重量的單據，還有開箱的照片，來佐證出貨短缺事實。通常賣方都會補短少的部分可是第二次補寄所產生的費用該由誰來負擔，這就需要與賣方爭取了。

Unit 23
供應商來訪

前情提要

Mr. Robinson 將到台灣訪問，兩位秘書們正積極地安排行程的內容。

人物角色

- Cherry　　　　Mr. Robinson 的秘書
- Jason　　　　 Mr. Tseng 的秘書
- Mr. Robinson　國外訪客
- Mr. Tseng　　 國內廠商

情境對話　

Cherry: Hello Jason, I was wondering whether Mr. Tseng would **be available** at 10：00 on 5th of July. Mr. Robinson would like to have a meeting with him to discuss the Da-Ling project. I will send you the agenda shortly.

佳麗：你好傑森，請問曾先生七月五日早上十點有空嗎？羅賓森先生想跟他討論一下大林專案，我晚一點把會議要討論的事項傳給你。

Jason: Let me check his schedule. He has a meeting booked with our sales manager that morning, is Mr. Robinson free that afternoon? Say 2 pm?

傑森：讓我看一下他的行程，嗯，他早上要跟我們的業務經理開會，羅賓森先生下午有空嗎？兩點好不好？

Cherry: He has a lunch meeting with someone else, and they should **be done** around 2 pm. Can you **book him in** for 3 pm then?

佳麗：他中午跟其他人有約，大概兩點會好，那約三點好嗎？

Jason: I sure can. Does he have a dinner plan? If not, I am sure Mr. Tseng would like to **take him out for dinner.**

傑森：當然可以，他晚餐有約人了嗎？不然曾先生想請他吃飯。

慣用語

1. be available 有空

Are you available this weekend?

你這個周末有空嗎？

---

2. book someone in 幫某人預約

Can you **book me in** for 10 o'clock tomorrow morning please?

你可以幫我約明天早上十點嗎？

---

3. be done (by / around) 結束、做完

Let's meet at 6 pm. I will **be done** by 5 : 30 pm.

我們約六點好嗎？我五點半就可以下班。

---

4. take someone out 請某人吃飯

Jason wants to **take me out** for dinner because I helped him with the project.

傑森説要請我吃晚飯，因為我上次幫他做那個專案。

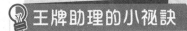 王牌助理的小祕訣

　　與國外客戶約見面，除了約會議時間之外，很多客戶會將要討論的事項（議程表）先通知對方，好讓對方有時間準備。如果對方是來介紹或說明新產品，不是屬於機密資料的話，也可以請對方先將內容提供給公司，主管如果有空可以先準備，有問題的話在會議上可以提出。一般台灣老闆都很好客，尤其是如果客戶是專程來拜訪公司的話，很多時候都會請客戶吃飯。

Unit 24
飛機延誤需更改行程及接機

前情提要

Mr. Rollings 預計來拜訪，可是飛機臨時延誤，他的助理 Tammy 趕緊通知對方公司。

人物角色

- Tammy　　　　　Mr. Rollings 的助理
- Mr. Rollings　　　國外訪客
- Frank　　　　　　國內公司秘書
- Mr. Wu　　　　　國內公司代表

情境對話

Tammy: Hi Frank, I am **sorry for** calling so late. I am calling to let you know that Mr. Rollings missed the connecting flight in Bangkok. They booked his flight for tomorrow morning, and he won't get in until 11: 00 am. Can you push the meeting back by a day and

潭美：你好法蘭克，很抱歉這麼晚給你打電話，我是想通知你羅倫斯先生在曼谷機場的班機沒接上，他們重新幫他訂了明天早上的飛機，可是他要早上 11 點才會

reschedule it to **the day after**?

Frank: Thanks for letting me know. from what I can recall, I think Mr. Wu would be free the day after. It should not be a problem. Can you let me know the flight number please? I will notify the driver, so he will **be there** to **pick him up** when he arrives.

到，可以麻煩你把原來的會議推遲一天改成後天嗎？

法蘭克：謝謝你通知我，我記得吳先生後天有空，應該沒有問題。可以告訴我他們班機號碼嗎？我會通知司機在他抵達機場時會去接他。

 **慣用語**

1. sorry for V+ing 為了某事道歉

Sorry for misplacing your sunglasses. I will get you a new one.

不好意思我把你的太陽眼鏡弄丟了，我會再買一個新的賠給你。

---

2. the day after 後天

He is coming to visit **the day after**. You'd better be prepared.

他後天會來訪，你要準備一下喔。

---

3. be there 出席

The meeting is on Thursday. Make sure you will **be there**.

星期四要開會，記得要去。

---

4. pick someone up 接某人

I will be free this afternoon. I can **pick him up** from the airport.

我今天下午有空，我可以去機場接他。

王牌助理的小祕訣

　　有時候計劃趕不上變化，就算是安排好的行程有時候還是會因為天氣或是人為的因素而要調整。如果是轉機的班機延誤的話，通常人都已經在半路了，修改也都很臨時，所以如果有國外訪客的話，提供手機號碼做連絡是必要的，助理們也要全程監控轉機過程還有台灣這裡接機司機的聯絡。最好是前一天或當天再次與司機聯絡以確保司機有準時到達並且有順利接到訪客。

Unit 25
討論會議中談論的事項執行進度

前情提要

　　Mr. Rollings 與 Mr. Wu 開完會後，Mr. Wu 答應要提供一些資料給他，Mr. Rollings 的助理打電話來催了。

人物角色

- Tammy　　　　　　Mr. Rollings 的助理
- Mr. Rollings　　　國外訪客
- Jimmy　　　　　　國內公司秘書
- Mr. Wu　　　　　　國內公司代表

情境對話　　🎧 MP3 25

Tammy: Hi Jimmy, has Mr. Wu spoken to you regarding the specifications of the Da-Ling project? **Apparently**, he told Mr. Rollings he will forward it to him.

潭美：蘇西您好，吳先生有沒有跟你說過關於大林專案的詳細計劃書？顯然，羅倫斯先生有跟吳先生提過專案會轉交給他。

Jimmy: Yes, I am **working on it** at the moment. There are a few amendments that need to be done and Mr. Wu also wants to add a few things in it. I should have it ready by next Tuesday.

Tammy: That would be great. Do you have a copy of the **meeting minutes** that I can have? Just in case I missed anything.

Jimmy: Definitely, I will send it to you straight away.

吉米：有的！我現在正在處理，不過還有點地方要修改，吳先生還有東西要新增，我應該下禮拜二就可以給你。

潭美：那太好了，我可以順便跟你要一份會議紀錄嗎？我可以對照一下，怕我疏忽掉其他的東西。

吉米：當然可以，這個我馬上就可以傳給你。

01
PART
國貿口說篇

02
PART
國貿寫作篇

 **慣用語**

1. **apparently** 沒錯、很顯然的、聽說

Apparently, he got into a fight with the manager yesterday. That is why he is not in today.

他今天沒來聽說是因為昨天跟經理吵了一架。

---

2. **working on something** 花時間處理

James has been working on this presentation since last Tuesday.

詹姆士從上星期二就一直在忙簡報的事。

---

3. **meeting minutes** 會議記錄

Who is taking the **meeting minutes** today?

今天的會議是輪到誰做紀錄？

---

4. **definitely** 一定、當然

This report is flawless. He **definitely** spent a lot of time on it.

這份報告做得盡善盡美，他一定花了很多時間來寫。

💡 王牌助理的小祕訣

　　助理的工作很廣泛，會議也是其中的一個重點。除了會議前的資料準備，開會時還要注意整理會議紀錄，依照會議紀錄的內容再去做後續的追蹤及處理。例如將特定的資料給某人，準備報表，或報價單之類的。別忘了對方的助理也需要一份會議紀錄，畢竟他可能不在現場，他更需要知道會議中討論過的事項，他也會有他需要跟進的事項。

Unit 26
訪客的喜好／注意事項

Mr. Moss 將到台灣拜訪客戶，他的助理 Belinda 正與對方公司的助理交代一些細節。

人物角色

• Mark　　　　　國內公司助理
• Belinda　　　　Mr. Moss 的助理
• Mr. Moss　　　國外公司代表

情境對話　 MP3 26

Mark: Hey Belinda, I am **making a reservation** for lunch for Mr. Moss. Does he have any special **dietary requirements**?

Belinda: No, he is pretty easy, but he does prefer a light lunch. **As much as** he enjoys Taiwanese

馬克：柏琳達您好，我現在要幫摩斯先生安排午餐的餐廳，請問他有沒有什麼東西不吃的？

柏琳達：沒有，他還蠻隨和的，但他中午習慣吃清淡一點。雖

food, he would prefer a sandwich and salad for lunch.

然他喜歡台菜，可是午餐他還是偏好吃三明治和沙拉。

Mark: Right, I think in that case I will book a western restaurant for lunch then. Is there **anything else** we can pre arrange for him?

馬克：好的，既然這樣的話那我中餐就訂西餐廳，還有什麼其他的事需要先幫他準備的嗎？

Belinda: Yes, he would prefer to stay in a smoking room actually. Would this be a problem?

柏琳達：有，可以麻煩你幫他訂可以抽菸的房間嗎？這會有問題嗎？

Mark: Well, I will check with the hotel, if not, I can find another hotel for him.

馬克：嗯，我來問一下飯店，如果不行的話我就幫他找另一間飯店。

 慣用語

1. make a reservation 預約

That café is very popular; you'd better **make a reservation**.

那間咖啡館很受歡迎，你最好要先預約。

---

2. dietary requirement 飲食的注意事項

He is allergic to seafood, and this is the only **dietary requirement**.

他飲食上唯一要注意的事就是他對海鮮過敏。

---

3. as much as 就算，儘管

As much as he wants to take part in this project, he still does not have enough qualification.

就算他真的很有心想參與這個專案，可是他還是資格不符。

---

4. anything else 其他的事項

Is there **anything else** you would like to add?

還有沒有其它要補充的部分？

王牌助理的小祕訣

　　外國人的飲食習慣的確與台灣人不同，尤其是午餐。如果午餐時間需要在公司用餐需要訂外食的話，不妨參考速食店或咖啡店。台式便當的份量對外國人來說稍嫌多了點。外國人都是輕食主義，三明治沙拉之類的他們會比較習慣。晚餐的話大部分都可以接受中式的餐點但是記得要問 *Dietary requirement*，因為不吃海鮮或是對海鮮過敏的人並不少。

Unit 27
與訪客確認行程

前情提要

Mr. Harvey 想要訪問台灣的代理商,他想要與代理商一起去拜訪幾個重要的客戶,他的助理 Yvonne 請代理商 Jimmy 幫忙訂行程。

人物角色

- Yvonne   Mr. Harvey 的助理
- Jimmy   國內代理商助理
- Mr. Harvey   國外總公司代表

情境對話

Yvonne: Hi Jimmy, I was wondering if Mr. Harvey's schedule to Taiwan is finalized?

伊凡:吉米您好,我想請問哈維先生的台灣的行程都定案了嗎?

Jimmy: <u>More or less</u>, his accommodations are confirmed. He is booked in to stay in Holiday

吉米:差不多了,飯店訂好了,他會在假日飯店住兩晚。司機

114

Inn for two nights. The driver will pick him up from the airport **the night of 25th**, and **take him to** the hotel. I am just waiting to **hear back from** this other client, to see if they are available in the morning of the 27th, then I will be able to send you the completed schedule.

Yvonne: Sounds good. Thank you very much for your help.

在 25 號晚上會去接他，然後帶他去飯店。我還在等他其他客戶的確認，看看他們是不是 27 號早上有空，然後我就可以傳一份行程表給你。

伊凡：太好了！謝謝你的幫忙。

 慣用語

1. more or less 差不多

These two items are **more or less** the same.

這兩項產品其實差不多。

---

2. the night of someday 某日的晚上

Would you like to go for a movie **the night of the 3ʳᵈ**?

三號晚上要不要去看電影？

---

3. take someone / something to somewhere 送某人／某物到某處

Can you **take this report to the office** for me, please?

可以麻煩你幫我把這份文件拿進辦公室嗎？

---

4. hear back from someone 等某人確認

I finally **heard back from Tina** that she will be available tomorrow.

緹娜終於跟我確認了，她說他明天有空。

王牌助理的小祕訣

　　代理商的角色就像國外總公司在台灣的分公司，所以如果有總公司的代表要到台灣來觀察市場或是拜訪客戶，那所有的參訪行程就會由台灣的代理商主導，行程上也會全程陪同。畢竟代理商跟客戶有直接的商業關係，總公司的代表通常是為了維持客戶關係或是推廣新產品才會來訪，可能與代理商也不常有機會見面，可以趁這個機會拉近跟總公司的距離。

Unit 28
廠商想直接拜訪客戶

((⚡)) 前情提要

　　Mr. Pence 是 Johnny 公司的一個供應商，他即將來訪台灣主要是拜訪其他的客戶，他知道 Johnny 公司有跟東盛公司做生意，他想藉這層關係去拜訪東盛公司。

👤 人物角色

• Mr. Pence　　　國外供應商
• Kelly　　　　　Mr. Pence 的助理
• Johnny　　　　台灣進口商

🎧 情境對話 MP3 28

Kelly: Hi Johnny, I know you are **in the process of** sorting of the schedule. I was wondering if it's possible to **set up a meeting** with Tung-Seng company. Mr. Pence would like to do a sales presentation on our latest model.

凱莉： 強尼您好，我知道你正在為我們的來訪做準備，我是想問你，有沒有機會可以跟東盛公司見個面，因為彭斯先生想跟他們介紹我們最新的設備。

Johnny: Well, I would have to check with Mrs. Lee first. She normally does not involve the supplier directly with our clients.

Kelly: It will be really helpful If you can check with Mrs. Lee. Mr. Pence believes it will **be beneficial**.

Johnny: Sure, I will check with her, but I will **be honest with you**, but is very unlikely.

強尼：這個嘛，我要先問一下李女士，因為通常她是不會帶廠商去見客戶的。

凱莉：好啊，那就麻煩你幫我們跟她溝通一下，因為彭斯先生覺得對商議上會很有幫助。

強尼：好的，我會幫你問，可是老實說，但是實在是不太可能。

慣用語

1. in the process of 正在處理、在某過程中

She is **in the process of** getting a divorce. I don't think she is in a good mood.

她正在處理離婚的手續，所以心情應該不太好。

---

2. set up something 安排

Can you help me to **set up** the PowerPoint system please?

你可以幫我安排做簡報的投影設備嗎？

---

3. beneficial 有好處

I think it would be very **beneficial** to have Tom onboard. He is an IT expert.

我覺得湯姆加入我們團隊是有助益的，他是個電腦高手。

---

4. be honest with someone 像某人坦承、老實跟某人說

To be honest with you, I don't think the promotion will come through.

老實說，我覺得升職的機會大概是沒有了。

王牌助理的小祕訣

　　如果是一般的進口商，偶爾也是會有國外的廠商來訪。可能是一向固定合作的供應商，或是之前有交易過的公司，剛好要來台灣也想看看是不是還有合作的機會。其實就算國外供應商知道使用者（End user）是誰，台灣進口商也不太可能帶供應商去認識客戶。畢竟兩方有利益衝突，如果供應商跟客戶直接搭上線，那受影響最大的就是進口商了。

Unit 29
私人觀光行程

前情提要

　　Mr. Harvey 希望在台灣出差的時候可以多留幾天到墾丁度假，他的助理請台灣的代理商幫忙訂行程。

人物角色

- Yvonne　　　　　Mr. Harvey 的助理
- Jimmy　　　　　國內代理商助理
- Mr. Harvey　　　國外總公司代表

情境對話

Yvonne: Thanks for **making all the appointments** for Mr. Harvey, and there is one more thing. Do you think you can book a couple of nights of accommodation in Kenting for him as well? He would like to **stay on** for a bit of holiday.

伊凡：謝謝你幫哈維先生安排行程，還有一件事要麻煩你，你可以幫他在墾丁定兩個晚上的住宿嗎？他想要順便度個假。

Jimmy: Not a problem, <u>**what kind of accommodation is he after**</u>?

Yvonne: He would prefer to stay in a resort type accommodation, price range between 150 EURO – 200 EURO per night.

Jimmy: Sure, there are lots to <u>**choose from**</u>. I will send you some information and you can let me know which one to book for him.

吉米：沒問題，他想要怎樣的房型？

伊凡：他喜歡住度假村類型飯店，預算大概是每個晚上 150 到 200 歐元左右。

吉米：好的，那他的選擇還不少，我再傳一些飯店的資料給你，你再跟我説要幫他訂哪一間。

01
PART
國
貿
口
説
篇

02
PART
國
貿
寫
作
篇

慣用語

1. make an appointment 預約

I need to **make an appointment** to see the dentist. My tooth is killing me.

我需要去看牙醫。我的牙痛到爆。

---

2. stay on 停留下來

All the work is done, but I will **stay on** a bit longer just to make sure the office is locked up properly.

工作都處理好了，可是我會留下來確認辦公室有沒有鎖好。

---

3. what is someone after 想要什麼

Do you know **what Mr. Thomson is after**?

你知道湯森先生找我做什麼嗎？

---

4. choose from 可供選擇

The range is very limited, so I don't have a lot to **choose from**.

新貨很少，所以我沒有幾項可以挑的。

王牌助理的小祕訣

　　很多國外的訪客都會趁出差的機會順便欣賞台灣的風光，通常如果是他們的私人行程，台灣的廠商是不用陪同的，頂多就是幫忙訂飯店或是觀光行程，只要將訂房或訂位紀錄交給對方助理即可。飯店通常可以接受入住後由房客付款，只是房價較高。某些飯店可能會要求先付訂金，如果有代墊的金額也記得要向訪客請款。或者幫訪客找飯店資料再請訪客助理上網訂房。

Unit 30
詢問工程師行程表

前情提要

　　Peggy 是 Dexter 公司在台灣的代理商，目前有個案子需要總公司派人來安裝，Peggy 向 Dexter 確認工程師的行程。

人物角色

- Peggy　　　台灣代理商
- Dexter　　　國外公司代表
- Andrew　　 國外工程師
- Clive　　　 國外工程師
- Mark　　　 國外工程師

情境對話　 MP3 30

Peggy: So do you know which engineers will be coming to do the installation yet?

佩琪：那你知道是哪幾個工程師會來安裝了嗎？

Dexter: Well, at the moment I got Andrew and Clive available, I know you prefer Mark, but he won't be

戴斯特：嗯，目前只有安德魯還有克萊夫有空，我知道你比較

available **until the end of May**. I don't think the end user can wait that long.

想要馬克去，可是他要到五月底才會有空。我不認為客戶能夠等這麼久。

Peggy: Yes, they are **in a bit of hurry**. I think Andrew and Clive are ok. How soon can they **get here**?

佩琪：是啊，他們是很急，我覺得安德魯和克萊夫也可以，他們最快什麼時候可以到？

Dexter: Andrew will be finishing his project in Korea at the end of next week. I can arrange them to arrive in Taipei on 5th of April.

戴斯特：安德魯下星期就會把韓國的案子做完，我可以安排他們四月五日抵達台北。

Peggy: Well, it is a **public holiday** here. Would you be able to change it to 6th April?

佩琪：可是那天是國定假日，不然如果日期改到四月六日如何呢？

1. until the end of Month 直到某月底

I won't be going away **until the end of March**.

我三月底才會去放假。

---

2. in a bit of hurry 有點著急

I am **in a bit of hurry**. Can you tell me how much longer I have to wait, please?

我有點趕時間,你可以告訴我還要等多久嗎?

---

3. get somewhere 到某處

Luckily, I got the GPS; otherwise, I would never **get there**.

還好我有 GPS,不然我一定到不了。

---

4. public holiday 國定假日

Ever since we got two days weekend, the amount of the **public holidays** has been reduced.

自從周休二日之後,國定假日的數量就減少了。

 王牌助理的小祕訣

　　如果是之前合作過的客戶，他們通常對來安裝的工程師會有偏好，有時候也會想指定某位工程師。或許是能力又或許是跟廠裡的員工之前有交情。可是工程師們手上有很多案子要做，無法按照客戶的要求，一切都要照公司的安排。日期上也要考慮是不是會卡到國定假日或是客戶方面人手的調度，畢竟有國外工程師在時，客戶也會需要安排人手來配合安裝工作。

Unit 31
零件延誤

 **前情提要**

　　此次的安裝工作有需要修改原來的過濾系統，可是修改過濾系統的零件目前還卡在海關，被抽驗。Peggy 想請工程師先做安裝的部分。

 **人物角色**

- Peggy　　　　　國內代理商
- Andrew　　　　國外工程師

 **情境對話**　🎧 MP3 31

Peggy: Did Dexter mention that other than the standard installation, we also need to replace the filter system?

佩琪：戴斯特有跟你提過除了標準的安裝工作之外，還要更換原來的過濾設備嗎？

Andrew: Yes, he did.

安德魯：有，他有提到。

Peggy: But **there is a slight delay**

佩琪：可是過濾設備

with the filter system parts. They **got stuck** in customs and will probably would take a few more days before they are released to us. Do you think you can start on the installation first and do the filter system later?

Andrew: I would prefer to do the filter system first, but I guess **there is no other way**. I just can't **sit around and do nothing**.

Peggy: Phew, thanks for that. I will be in so much trouble if you need those parts right away.

的零件有點延誤,目前卡在海關,可能還要好幾天才會發回給我們。你可以先著手開始安裝工作然後晚一點再做過濾設備嗎?

安德魯:我是希望先做過濾設備,可是現在也沒辦法,我總不能在這裡乾等。

佩琪:喔～你真是救星!如果你堅持要先做過濾設備的話那我就慘了。

 慣用語

1. **there is a slight delay** 有點小延誤

There is a slight delay with the high speed rail, so Daniel will be here in 10 mins.

高鐵有點小延誤，所以丹尼爾在十分鐘就會到。

---

2. **got stuck somewhere** 在某處卡住

The receipt **got stuck** in the crack, and I can't get it out.

收據被卡在細縫裡，而我拿不出來。

---

3. **there is no other way** 沒有其他方式了

I think we have to cancel the order because **there is no other way**.

我想我們也只能取消訂單了，真的沒有其他辦法了。

---

4. **sit around and do nothing** 浪費時間，不做事

I don't know how he can just **sit around and do nothing** the whole day. I am sure he will be fired soon.

他每天都在浪費時間不做事，他遲早會費開除。

王牌助理的小祕訣

　　安裝工作除了需要工程師執行之外，更需要配合零件來做必要的修改或更換。所以在大概知道何時要執行安裝工作前，務必確認需要的零件在工程師到工廠之前會先到台灣。萬一像情境對話中的情況，零件因為某些原因延誤，則可以先跟工程師商量，請工程師幫幫忙，從其他可以先做的地方先下手。這樣工程師不用浪費時間等候，畢竟他們也需要向總公司回報進度。

Unit 32
對工程師的提點

前情提要

　　Andrew 是第一次到台灣客戶這裡執行安裝工作，Peggy 正在跟他交代工廠裡面的一些文件如何填寫。

人物角色

- Peggy　　　台灣代理商
- Andrew　　國外工程師
- Mr. Kao　　客戶廠房裡的主管

 情境對話　 MP3 32

Peggy: Since this is the first time you work in this factory, there is **something you need to know**. There is a daily report that you need to **fill out** at the end of the day and make sure you get the department supervisor to sign it as well.

佩琪：既然這是你第一次到這個廠房做安裝，有些事情我需要跟你說明。下班前記得要填寫每日施工進度報告，還要記得給部門主管簽名。

Andrew: Okay, which one is the department supervisor?

安德魯：好的，那主管是哪一個？

Peggy: It is Mr. Kao. The skinny guy with glasses. He normally does the morning shift and finishes work around 3 pm. The best time **to catch him** will be around lunch.

佩琪：是高先生，就是那個瘦瘦戴眼鏡的那一個。他通常是輪早班，所以三點就下班了。最容易找到他的時間就是午餐時間。

Andrew: Sure, anything else I need to know?

安德魯：好的，還有什麼是我需要注意的嗎？

Peggy: If you need any small parts, just go to the Maintenance Department. They will **be happy to** assist you.

佩琪：如果你需要一些小零件，那就直接去找維修部，他們很樂意提供。

 慣用語

1. something someone needs to know 某人需要知道的事

There is **something you need to know** as a new employee. You have to sign in and out at the reception each day.

因為你是新進員工，有些事你需要知道。你每天都到櫃檯簽到和簽退。

---

2. fill out 填寫

There is a registration form to **fill out** before you start.

你開工之前要先填好登記表。

---

3. to catch someone 找到某人

Here you are. I have been trying **to catch you** the whole day.

終於找到你了，我已經找了你一整天。

---

4. be happy to 樂意

If you can cover my shift today, I **am happy to** work on the weekends.

如果你今天可以幫我代班的話，我周末可以來工作。

王牌助理的小祕訣

　　如果有外國工程師來執行安裝，有時候代理商也無法整天隨侍在側，這時工程師就要靠自己來跑一些流程。通常工廠裡會指派一位人員來配合工程師，也算是統籌安裝的工作。如果負責人員英語能力不好的話，那代理商需要到場協助翻譯的時間就多了。如果工程師與廠內人員溝通上沒有問題的話，那代理商只需要固定到廠房追蹤一下安裝進度即可。

Unit 33
工程師反應問題

前情提要

　　工程師在安裝時發現有一些電路零件也需要更換,他向代理商反應。

人物角色

- Andrew　　　國外工程師
- Peggy　　　　台灣代理商

情境對話　🎧 MP3 33

Andrew: Hello Peggy, I think the client will contact you shortly regarding placing an order for a set of parts. We are having a problem here. We discovered some of the electrical parts are **worn out**. We need to replace it; otherwise, it would not **work properly.**

安德魯: 佩琪您好,客戶應該馬上會跟你聯絡要訂一組零件,我們安裝上有些問題,我們發現有些電路零件已經都磨損了,那些一定要換,不然機器會出問題。

Peggy: Right. Do you have the part

佩琪: 好的,那你有

numbers? I can check whether the parts are in stock. If not, I will put in an urgent order for them.

零件號碼嗎？我可以查一下有沒有庫存，如果沒有我就趕快下個緊急訂單。

Andrew: Sure, it is FE104-12 and two other cables. I also **had them written down** and gave it to the installation supervisor.

安德魯：有，那是 FE104-12 和其他兩組接線，我也有把號碼寫下來，已經拿給安裝負責人了。

Peggy: Thanks for the heads up, I will **put the order through** once I hear from them.

佩琪：謝謝你先告訴我，他們跟我聯絡之後我會馬上下訂單。

慣用語

1. worn out 磨損

I need to get some new shoes. The old one is so **worn out**.

我該買新鞋了。舊的已經壞得差不多了。

---

2. work properly 可以正常使用

My phone is not **working properly**. Maybe I need to restart it.

我的手機有點怪怪的。我可能要重新開機。

---

3. have something written down 將某事寫下來

I can't memorize it. I need to **have the phone numbers written down.**

我的記憶力差，我需要把電話號碼寫下來。

---

4. thanks for the heads up 謝謝你先跟我通風報信

Thanks for the heads up. I didn't realize the manager was not happy with my performance.

謝謝偷偷跟我説，不然我根本不知道經理對我的表現很不滿。

王牌助理的小祕訣

　　工程師在安裝過程中常常會發現一些其他需要更換或是修改的組件。這些需要更換的零件通常是沒有包含在安裝的零件裡面，所以客戶則需要訂購零件來更換。如果只是簡單的更換動作，那工程師可能會幫客戶直接更換處理。如果是牽涉到複雜的修改動作，那工程師會請客戶聯絡代理商報價。因為牽涉到報價的問題，工程師也通常會先跟代理商或總公司打聲招呼。

前情提要

代理商跟工程師確認安裝進度，看何時可以安排試車驗收。

人物角色

- Peggy　　　　台灣代理商
- Andrew　　　國外工程師
- Mr. Chou　　台灣代理商的負責人

情境對話 MP3 34

Peggy: Hi Andrew. How is the installation going? Do you think we will be ready for the commissioning?

佩琪：安德魯您好，安裝一切都順利嗎？你覺得下禮拜可以準備試車了嗎？

Andrew: The installation is going well, but there is **a small hiccup** that needs to be fixed with the feeding system. We will do the commissioning **in a couple of**

安德魯：安裝蠻順利的，只是送料系統還有些有問題需要調整一下，我們兩天後會先試車，下禮拜就可

days, and if all **works out**, we will be ready for the final test run next week.

Peggy: That's good to know. Let me know how you go with the test run because Mr. Chou would like to be there for the final test run. I will organize for him to be there next week **if all goes to plan**.

以正式做驗收測試了。

佩琪：那太棒了！等試車完畢時麻煩你通知我一下，因為驗收測試的期間周先生想親自到場，如果一切順利的話，我就安排他下星期過去。

01
PART
國貿口說篇

02
PART
國貿寫作篇

1. a small hiccup 小問題

There is **a small hiccup**; otherwise, it would have been finished yesterday.

突然有點小問題,不然昨天就可以完工了。

---

2. in a couple of days 兩天後

I need to give a presentation for this project **in a couple of days**.

兩天後我需要為這個案子做簡報。

---

3. work out 如預期的一般,順利

I am glad the new job is **working out** for you.

很高興你的新工作一切都很順利。

---

4. if all goes to plan 如果順利的話

I will be in Taipei by Friday **if all goes to plan**.

如果順利的話我星期五之前就會到台北。

王牌助理的小祕訣

　　工程師等於是代理商在廠房裡的眼睛，當然也是同一陣線的夥伴。代理商可以從工程師口中了解安裝的整個進度，這樣在跟客戶討論安裝情況的時候才不會在狀況外。試車驗收是很重要的步驟，因為牽涉到結案與請款。所以在機器還沒有調整好的時候，沒有十足把握的話，不會貿然地安排驗收測試。要安排驗收測試時也一定要先跟客戶確認執行的日期。

Unit 35
通知供應廠已順利完工

前情提要

整個安裝過程已順利完成，台灣代理商向總公司報告進度。

人物角色

- Peggy　　　　台灣代理商
- Dexter　　　　國外公司代表

 **情境對話** MP3 35

Peggy: Hi Dexter. Good news for you. The installation is **all sorted** and the commissioning and the final acceptance run both went well. We are in the process of getting the paperwork done. The end user will sign the certificate of acceptance shortly.

Dexter: That's wonderful. So when do you think I can have the

佩琪：戴斯特您好，有個好消息跟你説，安裝已經完成了，試車還有驗收測試都很順利，我們目前正在處理相關的文件作業，客戶很快就會簽驗收證書了。

戴斯特：那太好了，那工程師什麼時候可

engineers back? They **got another project to attend to** in two weeks time.

Peggy: Well, they need to stay on for one more week to complete the staff training. If you need them back **right after** that, then you can arrange for them to **fly out** either next Friday night or Saturday morning.

以離開？他們兩星期後還有其他的安裝工作要做。

佩琪：這樣啊，他們還需要多留一個星期來做員工訓練，如果你很急著要他們回去，那就安排下星期五晚上或是星期六早上回去好了。

01
PART
國
貿
口
說
篇

02
PART
國
貿
寫
作
篇

1. all sorted 搞定了、完成了

My report is **all sorted**. I can hand it in tomorrow.

我的報表弄好了,明天可以呈上去了。

---

2. got something to attend to 有某事要忙

I am sorry I have to go now. I **got a meeting to attend to** at 3 pm.

抱歉我現在需要離開。我三點鐘要開會。

---

3. right after 立即,完成之後

I can get out of here **right after** and be at the restaurant at 7pm.

我做完後馬上就可以離開,七點就可以到餐廳。

---

4. fly out 離境

Toby is **flying out** in three days. He wants to spend some time travelling in Taiwan.

托比還有三天才會離境。他想在台灣觀光一下。

 王牌助理的小祕訣

　　總公司關心驗收結果的原因不只是請款的問題，因為工程師通常還有其他的安裝工作要執行，能早一天驗收他們就能早一天去做別的工作。通常需要安裝的工作也需要員工訓練，而工程師就需要負責提供員工訓練。訓練的內容及時間長短就要依照合約上的規定。代理商則需要為員工訓練留下紀錄（出席名單及訓練內容等等），以便最後結案時當作履約的證明。

Unit 36
通知國外客戶國定假日

前情提要

農曆年要到了，Nina 向國外客戶通知農曆新年放假的日期。

人物角色

- Nina　　　　　　國內廠商
- Sam　　　　　　國外客戶

情境對話　 MP3 36

Nina: Hi Sam. How was your Christmas and new year holiday?

妮娜：艾咪您好，你的聖誕和新年假期過得好嗎？

Sam: It was very nice, thank you.

山姆：很好，謝謝你。

Nina: It is our turn to have a break from work. We will **be closing for** Chinese New Year from the 28th Jan to 7th of Feb. We will reopen on

妮娜：那現在就換我們要去放假了，我們農曆新年會從一月二十八日開始放到二月

the 8th Feb. You might want to **make a note** in your diary. **Feel free** to call me on my cell phone **in case of emergency.**

七日，我們二月八日開始正式上班。你可能需要在日記上做註記，如果有急事的話可以打我的手機。

Sam: Thanks for the info. What do you do for Chinese New Year?

山姆：好的，謝謝你通知我，那你們農曆年都怎麼慶祝？

Nina: It is like your Christmas; just spend time with the family.

妮娜：就像你們的聖誕節啊，就是陪陪家人。

Sam: That sounds good! Have a wonderful new year.

山姆：那很棒啊！希望你有個愉快的新年。

慣用語

1. be closed for 因為某事而關閉

Sorry we are not able to offer hot meals today because the kitchen is closed for maintenance.

不好意思今天無法供應熱食，因為廚房在整修。

---

2. make a note 記下來

If anyone called for me, can you please make a note since I will be away for two days.

我這兩天不在，如果有人打電話找我，可以幫我記下來嗎？

---

3. feel free 不要客氣、請自便

Please feel free and help yourself with anything you want.

請不用客氣，想吃什麼請自己動手。

---

4. in case of emergency 有急事的話

Amy will be acting in my position, please contact her in case of emergency.

艾咪是我的職務代理人，如果有急事的話請找她。

王牌助理的小祕訣

　　公司放假是無可厚非的事，只是對於常常合作的客戶一定要先通知，而且就算放假時公司也應該有緊急聯絡人的機制，就算不太可能有緊急狀況，求個安心也好。如果有個人化的電子郵箱也應該設定假日自動回覆的功能。這樣客戶才不會因為聯絡不上而不停的打電話或是發郵件。也可以趁這個機會跟國外客戶寒暄一下拉近距離。

寫作是種表達，許多句型的複製和抄貼，可能省一時之快，但卻非長久之策。許多語句跟句型不見得合適使用在每個情境。

國貿寫作篇介紹了最基礎且最常見的狀況，從這36 篇書信中可以累積自己的寫作表達庫，在遇到類似情況時，以最道地且清晰的方式回應廠商、訪客和工程師，成為國貿達人。

Unit 1
公司簡介，客戶開發信（進口）

前情提要

　　七海公司在網路上發現一間新的海鮮出口商，進口部經理想要多了解一下是否可以有合作的機會，他發了公司簡介過去。

人物角色

• Sales manager　　對方公司業務部經理
• Jerry Chen　　　　七海公司進口部經理

信件內容

Dear sales manager,

　　My name is Jerry Chen, and I am the manager of Purchasing Department from Sevenseas company in Taiwan. Sevenseas company is a trading company specializing in live and frozen seafood importation. We are not only a buyer but also a distributor to the local hotels and restaurants in northern part of Taiwan such as Hyatt and the Taipei Marriott hotel etc. We supply **a wide range of** seafood sourced from local and the international suppliers. The items in high demand are:

Frozen cooked lobster
Baby octopus
Salmon roe
Tiger prawn

If you are able to offer the above items, please send us a quotation, we would love to hear from you. If your company is **specialized in** a different range of items, please send us a list of the items that are available. We are always on the look for new items with potentials.

Looking forward to hearing from you.

Regards,
Jerry Chen

中譯

銷售部經理您好，

　　我是傑瑞陳，是台灣七海公司的進口部經理。七海公司是一家專門進口活體及冷凍海鮮產品的公司，我們不只是進口商，也是供應北台灣餐廳及飯店海鮮產品的大盤商。我們的客戶包括凱悅飯店及台北萬豪酒店等等。我們提供多樣的由當地及國際的進口產品，我們熱賣的品項有：

熟凍龍蝦
小章魚
鮭魚卵
草蝦

　　如果貴公司可以提供以上產品，麻煩您幫我們報價，我們希望能參考您的價格。如果貴公司可以提供的項目不同，也希望您可以提供我們貴公司的產品項目表，我們也積極在開發有潛力的新產品。

　　期待貴公司的回信。

傑瑞陳　敬啟

王牌助理的小祕訣

　　貿易公司常常會上網尋找新的國外客戶或是供應商，有時候對方網站上的內容寫太廣義，實在沒有辦法確認他們是否會對公司的產品有興趣。這時候發業務開發信可能是最容易的辦法，但是因為沒有跟對方連絡過，只能將信件寫給對方的業務部門，信件也很容易石沉大海。為了避免做浪費時間做沒有意義的事，發完信之後最好再以電話聯絡。

慣用語

1. a wide range of 各式各樣的、多種的

We found a new supplier, who can supply **a wide range of** fish fillets.

我們找到一個新的供應商，他們可以提供不同種類的魚排。

----

2. specialize in 專門、專攻

Our company **specializes in** frozen seafood. We don't handle live ones.

我們公司只做冷凍海鮮，我們不做活海產。

Unit 2
公司簡介，客戶開發信（出口）

前情提要

　　富銘機械是一間專門生產食品業包裝生產線的公司，他們有自己的設計部門，還有工程師團隊負責安裝。

人物角色

● David Liu　　　　　銷售部門主管

📧信件內容

Dear Sir,

　　Greetings from Fu-Ming engineering company. We are an experienced designer and manufacturer for packaging and canning lines for food industry. We are **capable of** customizing the design to suit your unique specifications in filling, sealing canning and packing. We have a strong Engineering Department which is experienced in industrial projects, and will be able to offer the professional advices for your design and drafting.

Other than providing onsite installation and executing all mechanical and electrical installation tasks, our engineers will also provide adequate staff training including fundamental training on basic trouble shooting. A complete set of operation and maintenance manual **as well as** spare part manuals are included in each project.

We can guarantee our price is competitive without compromising the quality, since both design and manufacture are done in house. We are a reputable company with clients all over the world and we are looking forward to discussing with you regarding your possible future projects.

Best regard,
David Liu

中譯

您好，

富銘公司向您問好，我們是專門做食品包裝生產線機台的廠商，對於設計及機台製造很有經驗。

我們有能力客製化您的特殊需求，無論是裝填、密封、裝罐或是包裝的部分。我們專業的工程團隊可以在設計及製圖方面提供您最好的意見。

我們的安裝團隊會全權負責機械及電路方面的安裝工作，同時我們的工程師也會提供適當的人員訓練，包含基本的故障排除。所有的工程都會有專屬的操作及維修手冊還有零件手冊。

我們保證在品質第一的條件下我們的價格會很有競爭力，畢竟設計及製造都是由公司一手包辦。我們是一間商譽很好的公司，因為我們的客戶遍布全球。我們很希望有機會可以跟貴公司洽談您的下一個案子。

謝謝，
大衛·劉

王牌助理的小祕訣

寫客戶開發信的時候，可以用很自信的口吻來行銷公司，特別是如果有得獎或是有某些特殊認證的資格，可以特別強調。對於外國人來說自信是非常重要的，他們對華人文化的謙虛並不太認同，他們認為如果你有能力，為什麼不讓人知道。所以針對公司的強項可以提供例子來佐證，或是列出有合作過的大案子或是知名客戶，這對行銷公司很有幫助。

慣用語

1. capable of 有能力的

Shirley is **capable of** operating the program on her own.

雪莉有能力自己操作程式。

---

2. as well as 還有，也是

These items are on special, **as well as** the shoes from last season.

這些商品都在特價，還有那些過季的鞋子。

Unit 3
向新廠商詢價

　　台灣進口商想要跟國外新廠商購買一套機械設備,之前有先電話連絡過,可是有些場地上的限制需要跟供應商釐清,需要以圖面溝通。

人物角色

• Mr. Roland　　　國外業務部經理
• Wendy Wang　　英文／國貿秘書

信件內容

Dear Mr. Roland,

　　It was my pleasure to speak to you early on today. Further **referring to** our conversation, here I am sending you a copy of the floor plan to clarify some of our concerns. As you can see there is a pillar close to the center. Please ensure the conveyor positions in between the pillar and the walkway indicated on the drawing.

Although second thing we would like to clarify is the design of the conveyor, it is required by our client to have protective rails on both sides of the conveyor to stop the glass bottles from falling off the conveyor. The conveyor speed should be symphonized with the bottler.

As a result, we would like to ask you to quote a completed conveyor system with a human interface with above mentioned specifications. Please quote the installation cost and approximate duration required for installation.

Thanks & regards,
Wendy Wang

羅南先生您好：

　　很高興可以跟您通電話，如同我跟您提過的，附上場地的圖檔給您參考。您可以很清楚看到大約在中間的位置有一根柱子，所以輸送帶的位置需要放在柱子與走道之中的空間。

　　第二點，儘管我們還想要強調客戶有特別要求在輸送帶的兩側需要有護欄的設計，以免玻璃罐掉下去。還要特別注意輸送帶的速度需要與生產的速度同步調整。

　　基於這些理由，麻煩你幫我們報價一組完整的輸送系統包含人機介面。請將安裝費用還有安裝大概需要的時間。

　　謝謝，
　　溫蒂·王

王牌助理的小祕訣

　　某些產業的詢價單不是單純的問與答而已，是需要多加解釋，或是配合圖面來說明，尤其是需要客製化的產業例如機械，或是與設計相關的產業。電話裡面講不清楚的地方，可以用圖來溝通，這樣也比較不容易會錯意。收到報價單之後，可以在與供應商確認一次可能會有爭議性的地方。報價過程一定要小心謹慎，畢竟是客製化的東西，若是資訊不正確的話，可能要花大錢修改。

慣用語

1. refer to 參考、回朔到、意指

Referring back **to** what we just spoke about, I think we should go ahead with the decision.

回到我們剛談過的問題，我覺得我們應該就這樣執行。

---

2. as a result 因此、基於這個原因

The vessel has been delayed **as a result** of bad weather.

因為天氣不好，船班被延誤了。

Unit 4
報價給新客戶

前情提要

明美公司是專門做 LED 燈管外銷的公司，國外新客戶向明美公司詢價是否有專做特定尺寸的商品。

人物角色

- Mr. Elliot　　　　　國外詢價客戶
- Lilian Wu　　　　　英文／國貿秘書

信件內容

Dear Mr. Elliot,

Thanks for your enquiry number: A10-035 dated 25th Feb 2017. We are pleased to offer the below item for you.

Quotation number: LW201701153

Brand: Ming May

Product name: C range LED slim down light
Type number: C12BTD57
Input voltage: 110V or 240V
Dimension: 70mm×110mm×30mm
Quantity: 100 pieces
Price: USD 10.00 each
Delivery: 4 weeks upon receipt of purchase
order.

Remark:
1. Please note the input voltage comes in two different types. Please specify on your purchase order.
2. Payment terms: 100% payment **in advance** via T/T transfer upon receipt of order confirmation. (Please cover the bank charge as well)
Bank details below:
Bank name: Bank of Taiwan
Account name: Ming May Ltd company
Swift code: BKTWTWTP
Account number: 056 003 772311
3. Shipping method: Via customer UPS collect (Collect account number **to be advised**)
4. Handling and packing charge: USD 10.00 per order.

Please note all down-light products are under 5 years replacement guarantee.

Thanks & regards,
Lilian Wu

 中譯

艾利葉先生您好,

謝謝您 2017 年 2 月 25 日傳來的詢價單,單號:A10-035。我們很榮幸的可以向您報價以下商品,報價單號碼:LW201701153。

廠牌:明美
品名:C 系列超薄崁燈
型號:C12BTD57
輸入電源:110V 或 240V
尺寸:70mm×110mm×30mm
數量:100 個
價格:每個美金 10.00
交期:收到訂單 4 周後

註記：

1. 請注意輸入電源分為兩種，請在訂單上註明。

2. 付款條件：收到訂單確認書後以電匯方式全額付清（包含銀行費款費用），匯款明細如下：

   銀行：台灣銀行

   帳戶名稱：明美有限公司

   國際銀行代碼：BKTWTWTP

   銀行帳號：056 003 772311

3. 運送方式：透過 UPS 客戶運費自付帳號（請在訂單上通知帳號明細）

4. 包裝處理費：每筆美金 10.00

提醒您所有的崁燈系列商品都有五年的換貨保固。

謝謝，

莉莉安・吳

　　對於報價給新客戶，一定要小心行事。最好是將公司的規定都清楚的解釋一次，尤其是牽涉到價格及付款條件。例如很多公司對於新客戶規定新客戶需要在收到訂單確認書之後立即將款項付清，而舊客戶可能就會享有較寬鬆的付款條件。其次就是保固及退換貨的條件或是其他會產生的相關費用的情況，等收到款項才發現客戶沒有付銀行手續費的時候就太遲了。

慣用語

1. be pleased to 對...感到愉快或高興

We are very **pleased to** tell you that you are nominated as the Businessman of the Year.

我們很高興的告訴你你被提名為年度商業人士。

---

2. upon receipt of purchase order 收到訂單

Upon receipt of the **purchase order**, we need to act fast so that our suppliers will get their goods in time.

收到定單時，我們要立即行動，所以我們的供應商能及時拿到貨物。

---

3. in advance 提前

Can you notify me **in advance** for any meeting bookings, please? Otherwise, I won't be available.

如果要開會的話請提前通知我，不然我沒辦法出席。

----

4. to be advised 等候通知

Mr. Abbott has booked his flight, but where he would be staying is still **to be advised**.

亞伯特先生的航班訂好了，可是住哪裡還不知道。

Unit 5
產品缺貨或停產

前情提要

　　瓊斯先生向凱西的公司詢價一公噸的高山烏龍茶，但是公司可以提供的量不足。

人物角色

- Mr. Jones　　　　國外客戶
- Casey Yang　　　英文／國貿秘書

信件內容

Dear Mr. Jones,

　　Thanks for your enquiry no. K16100331 dated 5th of Jan 2017 regarding A grade high mountain Oolong tea. Due to **a series of** the bad weather events and extreme heat during our summer months, and quality and quantity of the tea have both been compromised. Unfortunately, we are unable to provide the quantity you enquired for at this stage. Please find our offer below:

300 kilograms of A grade high mountain Oolong tea at $80.00 per kilo

650 kilograms of B grade high mountain Oolong tea at $60.00 per kilo

Delivery: 5-6 weeks

I understand the price seems surprisingly high; however, please note there is a shortage in supply of high mountain Oolong tea this year. Therefore, **as an alternative,** we would like to suggest A grade Jasmine tea if you have a market for it. We are able to offer one ton of A grade Jasmine tea at $30.00 per kilo. Available for shipping immediately.

Thanks & regards,
Casey Yang

瓊斯先生您好，

　　謝謝您 2017 年 1 月 5 日有關 A 級高山烏龍茶的詢價單，詢價單號碼為：K16100331。因為一連串的天災再加上這個夏天特別的炎熱，烏龍茶的產量及品質都受到影響。很不幸的，我們目前無法提供您詢價的數量，請參考以下的報價：

300 公斤的 A 級高山烏龍茶，每公斤 80 美元

650 公斤的 A 級高山烏龍茶，每公斤 60 美元

交期：5-6 週

　　我了解這個價格高的嚇人，實在是因為高山烏龍茶的產量稀少。如果您願意退而求其次的話，我們可以提供一公噸的香片，每公斤只要三十美元而且可以立即出貨。

謝謝，

凱西‧楊

王牌助理的小祕訣

　　貿易公司常常會遇到缺貨或是數量不足的狀況，尤其是與食品、原物料、農產品等等這種靠天吃飯的產業。這個產業的客戶其實也了解這種供給與需求所帶來的價格浮動。與其在缺貨的情況下就不報價，不如利用這個情況，化危機為轉機報價替代品或是公司有庫存的商品，如果做得成買賣的話，更是兩全其美，老闆也會覺得你腦筋動得快！

慣用語

1. a series of 一連串的

I am feeling sad after hearing **a series of** tragedies happening to my friend.

我聽到我朋友發生一連串的慘事，我心情很不好。

----

2. as an alternative 換一個方式，替代方案

We can try to find another supplier **as an alternative** since they are unable to offer.

既然他們沒有辦法報價，那不如我們找另一個供應商

Unit 6
季節性產品促銷

前情提要

Julia 公司收到國外廠商促銷的通知，想要趁機會殺價。

人物角色

- Tanya   賣方
- Julia   買方

信件內容

Dear Tanya,

Thanks for your email, we are pleased to know the season of the California apricot is officially started. As you mentioned in your emailed dated 4th of May 2017, there are 2 tons of A grade white apricot in stock and we were wondering whether they were still available? We would like to place the order for 2 tons for A grade white apricot for immediate shipping and 2 tons of apricots every two weeks for the total of 8 batches of apricots if the price is right.

We understand the unit price quoted is USD 3 dollars per kilo. We would be happy to place the order of 16 tons if you can bring down the price to USD 2.5 dollars per kilo. Please consider our offer and let us know whether we should **go ahead with** the purchase order.

We are looking forward to hearing from you.

Thanks & regards,
Julia Huang

譚雅您好，

　　謝謝你的來信，我們很高興加州杏桃的產期正式開始了。在你 2017 年 5 月 4 日的郵件中您提到目前有兩公噸的 A 級加州白杏桃可以立即出貨，我們想請問目前是否還有現貨嗎？我們不只要訂這兩噸杏桃還希望每兩周可以再出兩噸的杏桃給我們，如果價格談得攏的話，我們一共要訂八批。

　　我知道貴公司的報價是每公斤三塊美金，如果可以降到每公斤 2.5 美金的話，我們會很樂意下訂單。麻煩您考慮一下再通知我們是否可以發訂單過去。

　　我們很期待您的回信。

　　謝謝，
　　茱莉亞·黃

王牌助理的小祕訣

　　因為是季節性的產品，如果是盛產的時候，供應商會積極的想脫手，這時也是進口商撿便宜的好機會。跟國外殺價可以直接了當地給他公司期望的價格，國外供應商有可能會接受，就算不能完全接受的話，也可能象徵性的降一些。語氣上並不需要太具脅迫性，畢竟買賣不成仁義在，公司還是可以尋找其他配合的供應商。

慣用語

1. go ahead with something 照這樣進行

Gina decided to **go ahead with** the wedding even though he cheated on her.

吉娜在發現她男朋友劈腿之後還是決定要跟他結婚。

----

2. looking forward to something 期待

Kelly and I are going to Fuji for a holiday. We are so **looking forward to** it.

我跟凱莉都好期待要去斐濟渡假。我們都很期待。

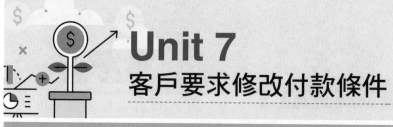

Unit 7
客戶要求修改付款條件

 前情提要

客戶傳郵件來要求修改付款條件，可是公司規定新客戶一律要下訂單後立即付款，因此跟客戶解釋。

人物角色

- Justin　　　　　　新客戶／買方
- Christine Le　　　賣方

信件內容

Dear Justin,

Thanks for your email dated 31th Jan 2017 regarding the payment term. In reply to your request, please allow me to explain our company policy to start with.

When it comes to new clients, it is a

requirement for all the new clients to pay in full upon receipt of order confirmation, and we enforce the policy strictly. Therefore, we are unable to revise our payment term on our quotation unfortunately.

I understand your frustration, and we would like to assist you as much as we can. We would like to offer you a better payment terms **from your second purchase onwards**, which is 30 % upon receipt of Order confirmation and 70% prior shipping. I hope this would suit your needs better. If you would like to discuss this further, please feel free to come to us.

Looking forward to hearing from you.

Thanks and regards,
Christine Le

親愛賈斯汀，

　　謝謝你 2017 年一月三十一日發過來由關於付款條件的電子郵件。請容許我藉由解釋公司規定的方式來回答您的問題。

　　如果是第一次合作的客戶，公司規定須要在收到訂單確認書後一次付清貨款。對於這個規定，公司一律嚴格執行，所以很抱歉我們無法修改報價單上的付款條件。

　　我能體會您的失望，我們也希望可以盡力配合您，所以從第二筆訂單開始我們可以給您更好的付款條件，下訂單時只需付三成的訂金，七成的尾款在出貨前付清即可。希望這可以幫上你的忙，如果您需要針對這個問題在討論的話，歡迎再與我們聯絡。

　　期待您的回覆

　　謝謝
　　克莉絲丁‧黎

 王牌助理的小祕訣

　　對於不熟悉尤其是第一次合作的客戶，一般公司的規定都是一定要下訂單時付款，很多國外的廠商甚至是每次訂購都是這樣的規定，除非有特別跟那家廠商談比較有利的付款條件。如果公司的現金流情況有困難的話，是可以跟廠商談談是否可以收到出貨通知再付款，或者可以詢問是否可以用信用卡的方式付款，這樣公司多一點時間可以周轉。

慣用語

1. when it comes to something 當談、說到到某事的時候

I always need Jerry's help **when it comes to** translation.

每次要翻譯東西的時候我就需要傑瑞來幫忙。

------

2. from something / sometime onwards 從某事／某時開始

The list price for all items will increase by 3% **from the next quarter onwards**.

從下一季開始所有品的牌價都將漲 **3%**。

Unit 8
確認報價內容及價格

Daphne 的公司向 Claudia 的公司詢價,在詢價時 Daphne 有特別註明需要照客戶要求包裝,但報價單上去沒有註明清楚。Daphne 再次向 Claudia 求證。

人物角色

- Daphne　　　　買方
- Claudia　　　　賣方

信件內容

Dear Claudia,

　　Thanks for your quotation no. LK4399-1 dated 4th April 2017. I am writing to confirm whether the price quoted includes the special packing requirements as we mentioned on our enquiry, since the packing requirement was not mentioned on the quotation itself and needed to be clarified.

Please note all items are required to be wrapped individually and boxed. The shipment is required **to be secured with a wooden crate** on a pallet. Both of the crate and the pallet **are required to** be fumigated.

The shipment will be transported directly from the port to the end user; therefore, please leave all shipping documents (ie: invoice and packing list and custom declaration) on the outside. We kindly ask you NOT to leave a copy of the invoice inside the carton.

Please kindly amend your quotation and confirm whether the packing requirement is noted and included in the unit price.

Thanks & regards,
Daphne Tseng

克勞蒂亞您好：

謝謝你 2017 年四月四日傳來的 LK4399-1 號報價單，我寫這封信的目的是想確認貴公司的報價是否包含了我們詢價內容中要求的特殊包裝方式？因為報價單上並沒有特別註明，我們覺得有必要澄清一下。

請注意每件商品都需要獨立包裝並裝盒。出貨時，貨物必須用木條釘箱並固定在棧板上。請注意木條及木箱都必須經過煙燻防蟲處理。

此外，麻煩您注意貨物進港後會直接送到客戶手上，所以請將海運必要的文件例如出貨單、包裝單及報關單存放在外箱上。尤其是出貨單絕對不能包在貨物裡面。

麻煩您再次修改您的報價單並確定您的單價已包含了特殊包裝的部分。

謝謝，
達芙妮‧曾

王牌助理的小祕訣

　　以進口公司來說，大部分的貨物在進口之後會由進口商再次包裝，然後再以公司的名義開出貨單給客戶。所以客戶不會知道商品的進口價格是多少，也不會去質疑進口商的利潤。但如果貨物很巨大或是很重的情況下，因為運送不易，通常在貨物到港後會直接由報關行跟貨運公司配合，直接送到客戶手上，公司再附上自己的出貨單。所以千萬要交代出口公司不要將文件附在商品裡。

慣用語

1. **secured items with something** 以某物固定

It is very windy today. You'd better **secure** the pot plants **with** ropes.

今天風很大，你最好把盆栽用繩子綁好。

----

2. **be required to** 必須、要配合

All the new employees **are required to** attend the training.

所有新進員工都需要去參加公司的訓練課程。

Unit 9
下訂單時註明將分批出貨

 前情提要

Maggie 的公司向 Sophie 的公司訂購一批水泥，因為大量訂購有數量折扣但 Maggie 公司並沒有倉儲的設備，所以要請 Sophie 的公司分兩次出貨。

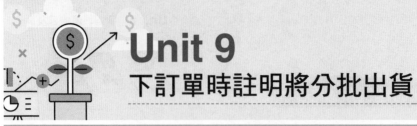 人物角色

• Maggie   買方
• Sophie   賣方

信件內容

Dear Sophie,

Thanks for your quotation number HA0991 dated 20th Feb 2017. We are interested in placing the order for 3 tons of 20 kilo bag cement since the **price is very compatible**.

However, we only go through about 1 and half tons of cement every 6 months and there is no storage facility available onsite. We were wondering whether it is possible to place the order for 3 tons for cement, but have the shipment divided into two 1.5 tons shipments every 6 month upon notification.

We are hoping this way we can secure the bulk buy price of 3 tons **instead of** placing two 1.5 ton orders at a higher price. We are happy to pay for 3 tons of cement in full upon receipt of your order confirmation.

Thank you and we are looking forward to hearing back from you.

Kind Regards,
Maggie Hsu

蘇菲您好，

　　謝謝你 2017 年二月二十日傳來的報價單，單號：HA0991。我們有興趣訂購三噸 20 公斤裝的水泥，因為價格實在很有競爭力。

　　可是，實際上我們每半年才能用掉 1.5 噸的水泥，而且我們並沒有倉儲的設備。我們想知道是不是有可能下單三噸的水泥可是幫我們每半年出貨 1.5 噸。出貨日期我們會再通知。

　　我們希望你們可以用三噸大量購買的價格來計價，而不是算成兩筆 1.5 噸的訂單，因為單價較高。我們願意在收到您訂購確認書之後，一次將貨款付清。

　　謝謝您，也期待您的回應。
　　瑪姬・徐

王牌助理的小祕訣

　　有些公司在報價時不但會依據客戶詢價的數量報價，還會主動將數量折扣報給客戶參考。就像是團購的概念，很多時候都會買越多越划算。進口商也可能會把團購價報給終端客戶參考。如果進口商本身就是用戶，而且又有倉儲的設備，那很可能一次買進做庫存備用。如果倉儲本身是個問題的話，跟賣方商量分批出貨，也是值得一試的好方法。

慣用語

1. something is compatible 某物很有競爭力、可相容的

The price of the computers is very compatible on their latest price list.

在他們最新的價格表上電腦的價格很有競爭力。

---

2. instead of 不如、除此之外

Instead of waiting for the customers to walk in to the store, why don't we approach them through social media?

除了等客戶上門之外，為什麼我們不主動用網路行銷？

Unit 10
需要追加數量，希望交期相同

(((前情提要

　　Audrey 的公司向 Josie 的公司訂購了三千個口罩，現在要追加到五千個，但是 Audrey 的公司希望賣方可以不要延長交期，盡快出貨給他們。

人物角色

- Josie　　　　　賣方
- Audrey　　　　買方

信件內容

Dear Josie,

　　Hope you have been well, I am writing regarding our order no. 10012 dated 4th March 2017. The order confirmation was received on 7th March 2017 to confirm the delivery of 6 weeks.

Since there is an urgent demand here, we would like to increase the quantity from 3000 pieces to 5000 pieces of masks. We are hoping that you will be able to deliver all 5000 pieces of masks in 6 weeks time as one shipment. As we just mentioned, there is an urgent demand; if we **missed out** the timing, the masks are going to be harder to sell. Therefore, we are kindly asking you to do us a favor and shorten the delivery **as much as possible**.

We understand there will be an additional cost for shipping, please charge it to our DHS collect account. And Once the delivery is confirmed, we will amend the order and send it through again.

Thanks and regards,
Audrey Chen

親愛的喬西：

　　希望您一切安好，我想跟您討論一下我 2017 年三月四日傳過去的 10012 號的訂單內容。我們 2017 年三月七日已經收到貴公司的訂單確認書，確認了交貨期是六周。

　　可是目前對於口罩有緊急需求，所以我們想加訂，將 3000 個改為 5000 個。我們希望貴公司還是可以在六周內一併將總數 5000 個口罩一起出貨給我們。如同我們剛才所述有急迫性的需求，如果我們錯過這個時機，那口罩就會很難賣了。因次我們懇請貴公司幫幫忙看看是否可以盡量縮短交期。

　　我們了解因為重量的關係，運費會增加。那就麻煩您直接以我們 DHS 的帳號扣款。等貴公司確認交期之後，我們會立刻修改訂單傳過去。

　　感謝您的幫忙。
　　奧黛莉・陳

王牌助理的小祕訣

　　對於已下訂單採購的商品作追加數量的動作並不少見，只是交貨期會是個問題。如果是賣方有現貨的話，那追加的量就可以直接出貨。但是如果是訂製品或是沒有現貨需要開生產線生產的話，那就可能會有問題。通常買方會想省運費，會要求賣方合併出貨，但是如果下單好一陣子了再來做追加的話，那原來的貨品可能就會因為要等追加的量而延誤出貨。若遇到此情形，公司要視情況做決定。

慣用語

1. miss out 錯過

I **missed out** on watching the basketball match because I was with a client.

我沒有看到球賽因為我跟客戶在一起。

----

2. as much / many as possible 盡可能的，越多越好

Linda told me to go find the old folders; she wants **as many as possible**.

琳達說要越多越好，所以她叫我去把舊的檔案夾找出來。

Unit 11
訂單內容錯誤，及時發現要求更正

前情提要

Erica 在收到賣方的訂單確認書後仔細確認，她發現確認書上的明細跟她想訂的東西不一樣，才發現原來她的訂單打錯了，她立即連絡賣方與賣方做更正。

人物角色

- Erica　　　　　買方
- Mindy　　　　　賣方

信件內容

Dear Mindy,

Thanks for your order confirmation for our order No. PO5564 dated 11th May 2017. Unfortunately, we spotted a mistake and would like to apologize for an error on our purchase order and we would like to **take this opportunity to** rectify it right now.

Please note there was a typing error for item 3, we are actually after the 220VAC solenoid valve, not the 110VAC. Please note what we **meant to** be ordering is:

Pneumatic solenoid valve part number: 4V20320A, 1/2 NPT, 220VAC×1 piece.

Please find our purchase order No. PO5564-1 attached. We have made the necessary amendments and part number for item 3 has been changed from 4V**1**0320A to 4V**2**0320A. Please kindly amend your order confirmation accordingly and kindly confirm the delivery.

Once again, we apologize for any inconvenience caused, and thank you in advance for your understanding and assistance.

Kind regards,
Erica Chiang

中譯

明蒂您好，

　　謝謝您 2017 年 5 月 11 日針對我們 PO5564 號訂單準備的訂單確認書。不好意思我們發現訂單上有個錯誤，我們寫信來的目的就是想針對這個問題做修正。

　　請注意，訂單上的第三項中有個字打錯了，我們需要的是 220V 交流電的電磁閥，並不是 110V 的。我們要訂的是：

　　氣壓電磁閥，型號：4V20320A, 1/2 NPT, 220VAC ×1 組

　　附上我們的訂單號碼 PO5564-1 供您參考，我們已經把第三項型號從 4V10320A 改成 4V20320A 了，麻煩您將貴公司的訂單確認書根據我們的訂單做修改，並且確認交期。

　　我們想再次向您致歉，也在此謝謝您的體諒及協助。

謝謝，
艾瑞卡・蔣

王牌助理的小祕訣

　　當收到賣方傳來的訂單確認書時，一定要再次核對訂單的內容是否與訂單相符，最好再與客戶的訂購單做對照。有時候不見得是對方的錯誤，也可能是自己本身打字上的失誤。姑且不論是誰的責任，重點是錯誤及時發現，而且立即被更正。零件的型號裡面常常暗藏密碼，例如 1 代表 110V，這方面就要對照零件的規格表，所以差一個數字就會差很多。

慣用語

1. take this opportunity to 趁這個機會

I would like to **take this opportunity to** thank Vanessa for her effort in this project.

我想趁這個機會謝謝凡妮莎對這的案子付出的心血。

---

2. meant to 應該要，註定的

I don't think we **meant to** take the right turn in the last intersection.

我覺得我們剛剛那個路口不應該右轉的。

Unit 12
出貨單上註明品名項目以利報關

May 的公司向 Alyson 的公司購買了一批零件,在收到 Alyson 公司的訂單確認書之後,May 發現所有的零件只有編號,並沒有將品名列出來。為了避免報關有問題,她請 Alyson 在文件上加註品名。

人物角色

- Alyson   賣方
- May   買方

信件內容

Dear Alyson:

Thanks for your order confirmation no. KK3342 dated 2nd July 2017. I noticed that all the items listed on the confirmation only indicated the correspondent part numbers, but all the product names are missing.

As we have **come across** problems with the customs questioning the documents and the shipments in a previous occasion. I was wondering whether you could do us a favor and kindly add the product name of each item on the order confirmation in order to avoid potential problems with the custom and duty.

For example,
Item 1. Part number: 104167-K3, Proximity switch×1

Please use above format on all exporting documents (ie: packing list and invoice) for all our orders and kindly amend your order confirmation accordingly. This would help us to **speed up** the importation clearance.

Thanks in advance for your assistance. Your help is highly appreciated.

Best regards,
May Ko

艾利森您好

　　謝謝你 2017 年七月二日傳來的訂單確認書，確認書號碼 KK3342。我發現確認書上的品項都只有型號，品項名稱都沒有打上去。

　　我們之前因為這種問題就遇到海關針對進口文件提出疑問。我希望你們可以協助我們，在訂單確認書上把品項名稱加上去來避免進口還有關稅的問題。

　　例如：
　　型號：104167-K3，近接開關一組

　　麻煩您在所有的進口文件上（例如包裝單及出貨單）都用以上的格式，也請貴公司一併更改訂單確認書。這對進口清關的速度會很有幫助。

　　謝謝您的協助。

　　美‧柯

王牌助理的小祕訣

　　有時候賣方的訂單確認書會太過精簡，雖然買賣雙方都能了解品項的內容，但是單據到了海關手上卻會產生很多問題。例如海關查驗時無法判斷是什麼商品，無法正確地選擇稅則，到最後還要與公司的進口部門聯絡，有時候還要臨時請賣方更改文件，實在耗時又費力。如果一開始就發現有這種情況，不如請國外配合一下直接將品名加註上去。

慣用語

1. come across 遇到、見到

I don't know how to solve the problem. I have never **come across** a situation like this.

我不知道要怎麼解決這個問題，我以前從來沒有遇過這種情況。

----

2. speed up 加速

I need to **speed up** the process because the end user needs the part urgently.

我需要加快處理的速度，因為客戶急著要這個零件。

Unit 13
匯款通知對方明細

Clarice 的公司向 Tracy 的公司購買商品，需要先付三成訂金。當 Clarice 完成匯款之後，她寫信通知 Tracy。

人物角色

- Clarice　　　　買方
- Tracy　　　　　賣方

信件內容

Dear Tracy,

Hope you have been well. I am writing to let you know the deposit for our purchase order No. 099123 has been made today. The amount of USD 3,000 has been wire transferred to your nominated account from our company account. Please find our company account detail below:

Bank of Taiwan
Payee: Han Lin enterprise
Account number: 94825-7899043

We have checked with Bank of Taiwan and they believe the payment will take about 3-5 days before the payment reaches your account. In the meantime, just in case if you wish to **follow up** with your bank regarding the payment, we have attached a copy of the T/T receipt for your reference.

The remaining balance of USD 7,000 will be transferred to you **upon receipt of** your notification prior shipment. Thanks for your patience and looking forward to hearing from you again.

Thanks & regards,
Clarice Lee

親愛的崔西，

　　希望您一切安好，我寫信的用意是想通知您我們 099123 號訂單的訂金今天已經付了。總共是美金 3000，已經匯到您指定的銀行，匯出帳號的明細如下：

　　台灣銀行
　　付款人：漢臨公司
　　帳號：94825-7899043

　　我們詢問過台灣銀行，他們指出款項應該 3-5 天就會到你們的帳戶。如果你想跟你的銀行追蹤款項的下落，可以參考我們附上的匯款水單。

　　剩下的 7000 美金尾款，我們將會在收到您出貨通知時幫您匯款。謝謝您的協助，期待您再次與我們聯絡。

　　謝謝，
　　克蘭詩・李

王牌助理的小祕訣

　　當完成匯款要通知國外賣方時，記得要附上匯款水單當作證明，尤其是需要賣方緊急出貨時。因為國際匯款通常都三到五天才會入帳到對方銀行帳戶，一般公司都願意接受銀行的匯款水單當作出貨的憑證，畢竟銀行有他的公信力，不太可能是偽造的。現在越來越多公司接受信用卡付款，如果沒有其他手續費用的話，信用卡可能比匯款更來得方便。

慣用語

1. **follow up** 追蹤，跟進，詢問

Can you get Sarah to **follow up** with the client, please? Apparently, they didn't place the order.

可以請沙菈跟客戶問一下嗎？他們並沒有下訂單給我們。

---

2. **upon receipt of something** 在收到某物之後

Can I pay cash **upon receipt of** the items, please?

我可以貨到付現金嗎？

Unit 14
廠商逾期未付款，催款

Zoe 公司收到 Helen 公司的訂單，也回傳了訂單確認書要求 Helen 公司匯款。可是等了一星期都沒有回應。Zoe 寫信向 Helen 催款。

人物角色

- Zoe　　　　　賣方
- Helen　　　　買方

信件內容

Dear Helen,

Hope you have been well. This is a friendly reminder regarding the outstanding payment for your purchase order 556332 dated 7th Aug 2017.

The order confirmation was emailed to you on

10th Aug 2017 with the instruction and the beneficiary details. Please kindly make the payment **at your earliest convenience**. Please note the order would only be processed upon receipt of payment in full. Please **take it into account** the delay of the payment would reflect on the delivery. We strongly advise to make the payment immediately.

Alternatively, we do accept credit card payment. Please note there will be 2% surcharge for all credit card transactions and American Express is not accepted. If you wish to go ahead with the credit card payment, it can be arranged.

Shall you require additional information regarding payments, please feel free to contact our account department on 9825 3713.

Thanks & regards,
Zoe Hsien

親愛的海倫，

　　希望您一切安好。這封信主要是想提醒你，貴公司 2017 年八月七日的 556332 號訂單仍尚未付款。

　　敝公司的訂單確認書已在 2017 年八月十日連同匯款的資料及收款人帳號一併給貴公司。麻煩您盡早匯款，請注意，所有訂單一律在收到款項之後才會入系統處理。特別是延遲付款還會造成交貨期的延誤。我們強力建議您盡快安排付款。

　　再者，您也可以用信用卡付款，請注意所有的信用卡交易都須徵收 2%的手續費，還要讓您知道，美國運通卡我們是不收的。如果您真的想用信用卡的話，我們可以安排。

　　如果您需要其他有關付款方面的資訊，麻煩您聯絡我們的會計部門，電話是：9825 3713。

　　謝謝，
　　柔伊・謝

王牌助理的小祕訣

　　某些公司對於匯款有比較多的規定，也許是統一作業的習慣，或是公司現金流的考量，所以並不是天天都會派會計去跑銀行，有時候要等上一星期或更久。如果有這種情況的話，可以跟賣方先打聲招呼，以避免賣方的疑慮。延遲匯款影響最大的就是交貨期，尤其是遇到要收到款項才會處理訂單的公司，建議匯款之後務必要再向賣方確認一下交期。

慣用語

1. at your earliest convenience 盡快

Getting this down **at your earliest convenience** would be like doing me a great favor!

你能盡快幫我處理就是幫大忙了！

----

2. take something into account 請注意、列入考慮的範圍

You need to **take the weather into account** if you are going camping.

你如果要去露營的話要注意一下天氣的變化。

Unit 15
請買方修改信用狀條款

 前情提要

　　Kimmy 的公司開了信用狀給 Lauren 的公司，當時在信用狀上並沒有註明可以分批裝運及轉運。但是因為後來船班的安排，貨物必須在新加坡轉運，所以 Lauren 請 Kimmy 幫忙修改信用狀。

 人物角色

- Kimmy　　　　買方
- Lauren　　　　賣方

 信件內容

Dear Kimmy,

　　Hope you have been well. I am writing regarding the Letter of Credit for your purchase order No. 667231 dated 3rd May 2017. We would like to discuss the current term of shipment. We believe it will be really helpful if you can change the condition for transshipment from NOT allowed to allowed.

The reason being, we are running into a few problems with finding the suitable vessel to port Keelung due to the global downturn, and there are fewer direct vessels available. If the transhipment is allowed, then our options are much wider.

There are 2 vessels leaving for port Singapore every week. Then there are 3 vessels heading to port Keelung from Singapore. The shipment will be able to reach port Keelung within 20 days. If you would rather wait for the direct vessel, then there is only one vessel every fortnight, which means it will take at least 35 days before the cargo arrives in port Keelung. Please let us know your decision.

Looking forward to hearing from you.

Much appreciated,
Lauren Hughes

親愛的琪咪：

　　希望你一切安好，我想跟你討論一下你 2017 年五月三日傳來的 667231 號訂單的信用狀問題，尤其是貨運條件的部分。我們認為如果您可以把船運條件從不接受轉運改成可接受轉運的話，事情會好處理很多。

　　原因是，因為全球經濟不景氣，直達的船班很少所以我們一直無法找到適合的船班，如果轉運是可以接受的話，那我們的選擇多很多。

　　目前每個禮拜都有兩班去新加坡的貨輪，然後從新加坡到基隆港的船班則一星期有三班，這樣的話商品大概 20 天之內就會到。如果貴公司寧願等直達的船班，那每兩個星期才會有一班，所以至少要 35 天才會到達基隆港。請貴公司考慮並指示該如何處理。

　　期待收到您的回覆，

　　謝謝，
　　蘿倫‧休斯

王牌助理的小祕訣

　　信用狀通常會用在金額較大的訂單，通常在開狀之前買賣雙方都會先協商信用狀理的條款。

慣用語

1. run into 遇見、撞到

I keep **running into** Johnny on the weekends.

我周末常常遇到強尼。

---

2. every fortnight 每兩個禮拜、14 天

The sales report is due **every fortnight**.

每兩個禮拜我都要交銷售報告。

Unit 16
廠商延遲出貨，要求賠償

前情提要

　　Sally 的公司向 Mr. Cunningham 的公司訂購商品，可是 Mr. Cunningham 的公司延誤了交貨期，導致 Sally 的公司被客戶罰款。Sally 的老闆決定寫信向 Mr. Cunningham 求償。

人物角色

- Sally　　　　　　　買方秘書
- M.J. Ma　　　　　　買方公司老闆
- Mr. Cunningham　　賣方老闆

信件內容

Dear Mr. Cunningham,

　　I hope you are well. I am writing to **express my frustration** regarding our order No. 77129 dated 3rd April 2017. The shipment was delayed by 5 weeks which caused a serious loss for the end

01
PART
國貿口說篇

02
PART
國貿寫作篇

user in their production line. We have; therefore, received a letter from the end user demanding to pay for the penalty for **breach of the sales contract**. The delayed penalty was set for 0.3% of the total sales value for each day of delay. With the total sales amount being USD 5,600, the daily penalty was USD 16.80. For 5 weeks which is 35 days, the total penalty came to USD 588.00

As we are not the party who caused the delay, we believe Cunningham & Co. should be responsible for the penalty. Therefore, we kindly ask you to refund USD 588 to us in order to cover our losses.

Shall you wish to discuss this issue further, please do not hesitate to contact us.

Best regards,
Sally Yeh on behalf of M. J. Ma

中譯

親愛的卡尼漢先生，

　　您好，我寫信的理由是想告訴您我對於我們 2017 年 4 月 3 日的 77129 號合約處理很不滿。我們的貨品遲了五個星期才交貨，這對我們客戶的生產線造成很大的損失。也因為這個問題，我們的客戶寄信來要求我們必須支付延誤交貨的罰款。每延遲一天，我們就須負擔銷售金額的千分之三。總價一共是美金 5600，這樣每天的罰款金額就是美金 16.80 元。那三十五天下來，罰款的總金額累積到美金 588.00。

　　因為延遲交貨並不是我們造成的錯誤，所以我們堅信卡尼漢公司應該要負擔這個罰款金額，我們在此要求卡尼漢公司退還美金 588 原來彌補我們的損失。

　　如果您想詳細討論這個問題的話，請隨時跟我們聯絡。

謝謝，
M.J.馬敬上（由莎莉・葉代筆）

王牌助理的小祕訣

　　通常和一般廠商或客戶連絡的事都是由助理來處理，但是如果牽涉到客訴或是要求償的問題，雖然仍是由助理處理，但卻會以部門主管或是公司負責人的名義來發信，來顯示事件的重要性。針對賠償的事宜，雙方展開很多討論及協商，會有很多書信往來，如果是用電話協商也需要事後用書信做回覆，把討論的內容寫上去，以免對方突然反悔。

慣用語

1. express someone's feeling 表達某人的感受

Words cannot **express how I feel** right now.

我真的不知道該講什麼。

------

2. breach of something 違犯某事（規定或合約）

I don't think you can park here; it is **breach of the traffic rules**.

車好像不能停這裡，這應該算違規交通規則。

Unit 17
折讓單金額抵貨款

Isabelle 的公司與 Gina 的公司的貨款是採月結制,而上個月因為退貨的關係 Gina 的公司出了折讓單給 Isabelle 的公司。這個月的貨款剛好可以直接拿來折扣。

人物角色

- Isabelle　　　　買方
- Gina　　　　　賣方

信件內容

Dear Gina,

Greetings, I am writing regarding the payment for our PO No. 34058 dated 11ᵗʰ Jun 2017; your invoice No. KK215590. The Current outstanding amount is EUR 3,895.00 and we would like to use our credit note against this invoice. Please find the copy of the credit note no. CD231 attached, the credit note amount is EUR 2,500. This should **bring down** the outstanding amount to EUR 1,395.00

With the remaining balance, we would like to pay it through wire transfer. The payment of EUR 3195.00 has been scheduled for next Monday, EUR 1395 is to cover the outstanding amount and the rest of EUR1,800.00 is to cover the invoice no. KK215556 dated 20th April 2017.

A copy of the T/T receipt will be forwarded to you once the payment is made. Please notify your account department **on our behalf** accordingly.

Thanks & regards,
Isabelle Lu

親愛的吉娜，

　　先跟您問個好，我是寫信來通知您有關我們 2017 年六月十一日的 P.O 34058 號訂單，貴公司的帳單號碼 KK215590。這個訂單的欠款金額是歐元 3895 元，我們想用折讓單來抵部分的貨款，附上貴公司的 CD231 號折讓單供您參考，折讓單的金額為歐元 2500 元。這樣還剩餘額歐元 1395 元須支付。

　　剩餘的款項我們會電匯過去給您，我們下星期會支付歐元 3195 元，其中的 1395 元是償還剩餘的尾款，另外的 1800 原則是支付貴公司 2017 年 4 月 17 日 KK215556 號的請款單。

　　匯款水單會在匯款之後傳過去給您，麻煩您幫我們轉交給貴公司的會計部門。

　　謝謝，
　　伊莎貝兒‧盧

王牌助理的小祕訣

　　對於常有在往來的公司，帳單通常是月結，所以一筆匯款內常包含幾筆不同的帳單。所以匯款之後務必通知對方匯款金額中所包含的帳單號碼及金額。如果之前有因某些原因有退款或是賠償的金額，因為有經常性的往來，對方可以直接開（Credit note）給對方，在下個月結帳的金額中直接扣除，這樣對方也不需要再花一次匯款的手續費。

慣用語

1. bring down 降低、拉下來

With Holly's sales figure so low, it is going to **bring down** the average.

荷莉的業績這麼差，會影響到大家的平均數。

----

2. on someone's behalf / on behalf of someone 代表某人、幫某人出面

Jimmy will sign the contract with T-J enterprise **on behalf of** the company.

吉米會代表公司跟 T-J 集團簽合約。

Unit 18
國外銀行扣手續費導致貨款不足

((♪)) 前情提要

Felicity 的公司在收到 Megan 的公司匯款之後，發現 Megan 的公司沒有支付銀行的匯款手續費，所以 Felicity 的公司收到的貨款缺了 27 塊澳幣，她即刻通知 Megan 的公司。

👤 人物角色

- Felicity Cooper　　賣方
- Megan　　　　　　買方

✉ 信件內容

Dear Megan,

Thanks for the proof of payment against our invoice number No. 16762 dated 2nd Feb 2017. However, we only received AUD 1,873 instead of AUD 1,900. The bank has advised that the fees are **deducted from** the total payment which caused the shortage of AUD 27 dollars. Unfortunately, we are unable to ship out your order until the full amount is received.

We understand AUD 27 is not a significant amount; therefore, we would like to offer you **the option of** paying with the credit card to avoid the costly bank fees. However, please note there is a 3% surcharge for all credit card transactions, and with 27 dollars, the surcharge is approximately 80 cents which is significantly lower than bank fees. And with the payment received immediately, we can ship out your order as soon as the transaction is approved.

Please let us know how you wish to process the payment.

Thanks & regards,
Felicity Cooper

親愛的梅根，

　　謝謝您針對貴公司 2017 年二月二日 16762 號訂單傳來的付款證明，可是我必須通知您，雖然您匯了澳幣 1900 元，可是實際上我們只有收到 1873 元，銀行告訴我這不足的 27 元澳幣是額外扣除的匯款手續費。很不好意思貴公司必須補足貨款我們才能幫您出貨。

　　我們了解 27 塊澳幣並不是很大的金額，所以我們建議您可以用信用卡付款以避免高額的匯款手續費。但是我仍要通知您，信用卡付款會有百分之三的手續費。對於 27 塊澳幣來說，手續費大概不過 8 毛錢澳幣，這跟銀行匯款手續費相比，實在低很多。而且在刷卡交易完成後我們可以立即幫您出貨。

　　請讓我們知道貴公司想如何處理。

謝謝
荷莉絲提‧古柏

王牌助理的小祕訣

　　處理國外匯款的時候，一定要特別注意手續費的部分。某些公司會在請款單或是訂單確認書上明確註明買方需負擔賣方所有手續費，如果是這種情況，務必要交代銀行國內外的手續費都要付，否則國外銀行會直接從匯款金額中扣除手續費後再撥款給賣家。如果貨款的金額不大，其實可以參考信用卡付款的方式，信用卡的費用可能沒有電匯的手續費來的高。

慣用語

1. **deduct from** 扣除

The monthly insurance premium is **deducted from** my account automatically.

我的保險月費會自動從我的帳戶扣款。

----

2. **the option of** 選擇

There is **the option of** paying the installment if that helps your financial situation.

如果對你的財務狀況有幫助的話，你也可以分期付款。

Unit 19
催促廠商出貨

前情提要

Ivy 的公司向 Elisabeth 公司訂購商品，訂貨時交貨期是確認為 8-10 周。從下訂單那天算起也差不多八週了，所以 Ivy 寫信向對方公司提醒及確認交貨期。

人物角色

- Elizabeth　　　賣方
- Ivy　　　　　　買方

信件內容

Dear Elisabeth,

It has been a while since we last spoke. Hope you have been well.

The delivery for our P.O. number 83289 is coming up fast. I was wondering whether the shipment was nearly ready for pick up? The order was placed on 2nd Feb 2017 and it has been 8 weeks since the date the order was placed.

For your information, our contracted delivery with the end user is 1st of Jun 2017, and the shipping time would take approximately 4 weeks. And with **2 weeks leeway,** the shipment has to be shipped out by mid April at the latest.

Please find our forwarder contact details below:

Tai-Euro forwarding company
Person of contact: Ms. Anke Muller
Phone number: +49 8370 0977

I believe Ms. Muller will be contacting you shortly since they are aware the delivery will **fall between** beginning of Aril to mid April.

Looking forward to hearing from you.

Thanks & regards,
Ivy Chen.

親愛的伊莉莎白：

　　有一段時間沒跟你聯絡了，希望你一切都好。

　　有關 83289 號的訂單的交貨期，時間過得真快，我想是不是大概快好了？訂單是 2017 年二月二號下的，現在也差不多過了八星期了。

　　我想要讓您知道，我們跟客戶的合約交貨期是 2017 年六月一日，船運大概要四周，再加上兩周的緩衝期，我的貨最晚四月中一定要好。

　　我們的船運公司的聯絡明細如下：
台歐海運公司
聯絡人：安卡・穆勒小姐
電話：+49 8370 0977

　　我相信穆勒小姐很快就會跟您聯絡，因為她知道交貨期大概是在四月初到四月中左右。

　　期待您的回應。

　　艾菲・陳

🔆 王牌助理的小祕訣

下了訂單之後，對於交貨期一定要特別注意，畢竟不是每個賣方都會站在進口商的立場所以想要小心地避免延遲交貨的罰款。所以最好的方式就是提前提醒賣方交貨期已經快到了。雖然有時候無論買方怎麼提醒，賣方不一定會理會，如果對方真的沒有回應，記得一定要及時反應給主管，至少在扮演助理的角色上已經盡追蹤的責任了。

慣用語

1. (length of time) leeway 緩衝、餘地

Is it possible to give me **a few more days leeway** please? I just got caught up with other things.

可以再給我幾天時間緩衝嗎？我最近在忙別的事。

----

2. fall between 大約落在

It is just an estimation; I think the score will **fall between** 50-55.

這只是我的臆測，我覺得分數大概會落在 **50-55** 分之間。

Unit 20
通知客戶需延遲出貨

 前情提要

Serena 的公司向 Carole 的公司訂購商品，可是下了訂單沒多久後，Carole 的公司向 Serena 反應將會延遲出貨。

人物角色

- Serena　　　　買方
- Carole　　　　賣方

信件內容

Dear Serena,

Hope you have been well. Unfortunately, I have a bad news for you regarding delay shipment for your order No. 55719.

We understand the lead time was originally confirmed as 6-8 weeks. However, due to the

234

unexpected shortage of the raw material, we are unable to start the production until early next month. This would cause approximately 4 weeks delay, we have to revise the delivery for your order to 12 weeks excluding the shipping time.

We apologise for the inconvenience caused, and please kindly notify the end user. Please **keep it in mind** that we have expressed our concern to the material supplier; however, at the moment they are not able to shorten the estimated delivery, we will keep pushing it. **If the situation improves,** we will be able to produce the order for you earlier.

Once again, we apologise for any inconvenience caused. We will keep you posted with further updates.

Thanks & regards,
Carole Lin

親愛的莎琳娜，

　　希望你一切都安好。不好意思我有個關於 55719 號訂單的壞消息要告訴你。

　　我知道我們先前跟您確認的交貨期是 6-8 周，可是因為突發性的原料短缺，我們要到下個月初才能開始生產貴公司的訂單，這樣的話會造成大概四星期的延誤，我們必須把交貨期更改為 12 周，海運的時間必須外加上去。

　　我們對於所造成的延誤深感抱歉，麻煩您先與用戶溝通。我們也向原料供應商施壓了，可是目前他們實在無法提前供貨給我們。我們會持續與他們溝通，如果情況有改善的話，我們就可以提早出貨給您。

　　我們希望再一次的跟您致歉，我們會隨時向您報告最新的動態。

　　謝謝，
　　凱若・林

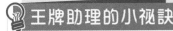 王牌助理的小祕訣

　　對於這種突發性的原料短缺所造成的交貨期延誤，說實在的除了提早通知買家讓他們可以有時間去調整或準備如何面對終端的客戶，因延誤而被罰款的事實很可能無法避免，但是至少賣方已經做到盡早告知的道義責任了。如果是進口商遇到這種情況，只能試著跟終端客戶溝通，如果真的面臨罰款的窘境，可以盡量與客戶協商，看是否可以減輕罰款的金額。

慣用語

1. keep something in mind 請注意、請記得

Please **keep that in mind**, you need to be there before 8 am tomorrow morning.

請記得明天早上八點前要到。

---

2. if the situation improves 如果情況有改善的話

He could be discharged from the hospital tomorrow **if the situation improves**.

如果情況有改善的話，他明天就可以出院了。

Unit 21
對於外箱標示有疑問

Becky 在協助客戶卸貨的時候發現木箱外註明的機器號碼跟文件上的有出入，因為還沒有辦法開木箱，所以只好先向原廠求證是否只是外箱上的錯誤。

人物角色

- Marcus   原廠聯絡窗口
- Becky   台灣代理商

信件內容

Dear Marcus,

Hope you are well. There is an emergency regarding the installation project in Pin-Tong factory.

The cargo arrived in the factory yesterday, and

while we were offloading to verify the content, we noticed that one of marking on the wooden cargo crate was quite questionable. On the marking it stated Model 461, machine number 23421. The machine number does not **line up** with the rest of the machines. We are hoping it is just a simple mislabeling mistake and because the wooden crate would not **come off** until Monday, there is no way we can verify what the content is until then.

Would you be able to check your record and see if you can find out which machine is actually in the crate ASAP please? We would have to make some arrangement if the wrong machine was delivered.

Best regards,
Becky Liu

 中譯

親愛的馬克思：

您好，有件與屏東廠相關的急事需要跟您求證。

貨櫃昨天到廠房了，而當我們在卸貨查驗內容的時候，我們發現其中一櫃的木箱上註明的明細有點問題。外箱上註明的是 M461 型的機台，型號是 23421。這個型號與其他機台的型號不連貫，我們希望只是外箱標錯了，可是我們要等星期一拆木箱的時候才可以對裡面的型號。

可以麻煩您盡快查一下你的紀錄看一下木箱裡的是哪一台機器嗎？如果機器真的出錯的話那我們要即刻安排後續換貨的事宜。

謝謝，
貝琪・劉

王牌助理的小祕訣

　　收到貨的第一個動作就是對照貨物及出貨單內容是否相符，當外箱的備註與文件上的不符合，這是第一個警訊。在無法開箱檢驗時，最好的方式就是回到出貨的源頭，找供應商確認。如果只是標示錯誤，那就大事化小。可是如果真的出錯了貨，那就必須退或更換，不但會造成交期延誤，原本安排的安裝工作也需要延期或暫停，有很多後續需要處理。

慣用語

1. line up 配合、銜接的上、等著

Ronald is trying to arrange a meeting with me, but our schedule just doesn't **line up**.

雷諾一直想跟我約見面，可是我們的行程怎麼樣都配合不了。

----

2. come off 卸下、掉下來

I was really embarrassed when the top button **came off** my shirt.

我襯衫最上面的那顆扣子突然掉下來，真是讓我丟臉死了。

Unit 22
供應商出錯貨

Melinda 的公司向 Francesca 的公司訂了一批修改案的零件，可是零件到了客戶的手上才發現國外可能送錯零件了，因為裝不上去。Melina 趕快請 Francesca 求證。

人物角色

- Francesca　　　國外聯絡窗口
- Melinda　　　　台灣廠商

信件內容

Dear Francesca,

Hope you have been well. I am writing regarding the shipment we received last Friday against our PO number 667113.

The shipment was delivered to the end user,

and they have tried to install the parts on to the machine; however, they are having numerous problems to identify the right parts for this conversion. We also pull out the part list for machine number KK350, and some of the parts that you delivered were not even meant for KK350, such as part number 1983773.

We highly suspect that this is not the correct shipment for our order PO number 667113. The description on the packing list was very general, which is listetd as "One set of parts for heating element conversion," therefore, we are unable to identify whether they are the correct parts of this conversion.

Please refer to the attachment. We **put together** a list with all the parts that we are having problem with. Please kindly check your record and inventory and let us know **what steps to take** next.

Thanks & regards,
Melinda Chang

親愛的凡琪斯卡，

　　您好，我寫信的目的是想跟您反應我們上星期五收到的 667113 號訂單。

　　零件已經送到客戶那而他們也開始安裝了，可是問題不斷，他們一直找不出這個修改案需要的零件。我們把 KK350 的零件單拿出來看，可是你寄來的零件裡有很多零件單上都沒有的零件，例如零件號碼：1983773。

　　我們高度懷疑這批零件不是給我們的 667113 號訂單，因為文件上形容得很簡略，只有説一組加熱設備的修改零件，所以我們也無法判斷到底是不是正確的修改零件。

　　請參考附件，我們將那些有問題的零件列表出來供您參考，請對照一下你的紀錄還有存貨，再通知我們該如何處理。

　　謝謝，
　　瑪琳達‧張

王牌助理的小祕訣

　　出錯貨這種事再所難免，只是有的訂單很清楚就就可以知道貨物不對，例如零件號碼不對，或是內容物不符。可是如果是一批修改零件而且又是由客戶們自行安裝，那可能需要一段時間才能肯定，到底是因為客戶不懂得如何安裝，或是來的零件根本不對。這要特別注意一下有沒有延遲交貨違約的問題，有的終端客戶會以收到正確零件時算起。

慣用語

1. put together 總裝、整合

We **put together** a small gift set for Jenny to congratulate her on her promotion.

我們大家選了幾項小禮物給珍妮來恭喜她升職了。

----

2. what steps to take 該怎麼處理、該怎麼做

I am not sure **what steps to take** in a situation like this.

這種情況我真的不知道跟如何處理。

Unit 23
查證出錯貨，立即處理

在 Melinda 向 Francesca 反應出錯貨的問題，Francesca 查證了之後發現真的是出錯貨。

人物角色

- Melinda 　　　　台灣廠商
- Francesca 　　　國外連絡窗口

信件內容

Dear Melinda,

Thanks for your email dated 8th July 2017 regarding the possible wrong items that were delivered. After checking with our clients and our inventory record, and it is confirmed that there is a **mix-up** with your order and the order for our client in Japan. Please accept our apology.

The shipment for you is in the process of being returned from our Japanese client as we speak, and we are asking you to kindly do the same and return the wrong shipment back to us **at your earliest convenience**.

Please kindly pack the parts in its original box and kindly contact HPS courier service to pick up the order under our HPS collect account. Please use our packing list as reference for the list of the product name. As for invoice, we are kindly asking you to put 1.00 USD as the value for each item to avoid paying for import duty. Please also put below remark on the invoice "Return for exchange".

Please accept our sincere apology. Your correct order will be shipped out to you as soon as possible.

Thanks & regards,
Francesca Ferguson

親愛的瑪琳達，

謝謝您 2017 年 7 月 8 日有關錯誤零件的來信，在我們跟幾個客戶查證還有對照我們的出貨紀錄，我可以確認貴公司的貨跟我們日本客戶的貨真的搞錯了。請接受我們道歉。

我們已經聯絡了日本的客戶，此時他們已經在處理退貨的事了，我們也希望您可以儘快將零件退回來。

請把零件裝回原來的箱子再請 HPS 快遞公司我們的付款帳戶退回來，品名的話請參考我們的包裝單，而請款單上麻煩你將每個品項的金額調整成 1 元美金，來避免進口關稅。在麻煩你再請款單上打上"退回換貨"的字樣。

我們真的很抱歉，貴公司的零件也會儘快出貨給您。

謝謝，
凡琪斯卡‧佛格森

　　如果需要將商品退貨或是換貨的時候，記得出口的文件上要註明，而且最好將金額降低，避免對方被徵收進口稅。而貨物再次進口的時候買方也可能再次被收一次進口稅，所以相關的單據要保留，而再次進口也最好在文件上註明是換貨的原因，這可以跟海關反應。否則抽兩次關稅，又延誤了交貨期，公司該有的利潤也都損失了。

慣用語

1. **mix-up** 搞錯、失誤

There was a **mix-up** with our hotel booking, so they have us booked in for only one night.

飯店把我們的訂房紀錄搞錯了，所以他們說我們只有訂一晚。

---

2. **at someone's earliest convenience** 盡快、盡早

It will be great if you can get this done **at your earliest convenience**.

如果你可以儘早處理這件事那就太棒了。

Unit 24
商品品質不良，要求換貨

前情提要

Penny 公司向 Evelyn 的公司購買燈管，可是到貨時卻發現有很多破損的，Penny 立刻向 Evelyn 反應。

人物角色

- Penny   買方
- Evelyn   賣方

信件內容

Dear Penny,

Greetings, I am writing regarding the shipment that we received for our PO number 333860 dated 3rd May 2017.

We received 100 ring lamps in this shipment; however, after we opened the boxes and inspected the lamps, we realized there are 17 broken lamps which we are not able to sell. Please kindly check your inventory and see if you have 17 pieces in stock. The end user needs these lamps urgently; we are **under tight deadlines**.

Please kindly let us know whether it is required to have the broken lamps to be couriered back to you for exchange. We would like to suggest that instead of shipping the broken lamps back, we can take a photo to show you as **proof of** damage in order to save the postage. Please kindly confirm whether this is acceptable.

Your prompt reply is highly appreciated.

Best regards,
Evelyn Hu

親愛的潘妮，

　　先跟您問聲好，我這封信主要的目的是想要跟你討論我們 2017 年 5 月 3 日下的 333860 號訂單所收到的貨品。

　　我們收到了 100 之的環形燈管，可是當我們開箱檢查時發現其中有 17 支燈管都是破損的狀態，我們沒有辦法賣給客戶。麻煩您查一下是不是有 17 支的庫存，客戶急需這些燈管，我們的交貨期很緊迫。

　　麻煩您確認這些破損的燈管還要不要寄回去給你換貨，我們是建議不如就拍照給你看，當作是損壞的證明，因為如果寄回去給您的話，也是浪費郵資。請您確認這樣是否可行。

　　期待您儘快回覆，

　　謝謝，
　　伊芙琳‧胡

 王牌助理的小祕訣

　　如果是像燈管這種易碎品，很多出口商在某一個限額內（例如 10%的數量）都會願意再次出貨，但不見得是無償補給買家，很多廠商會在限額內以折扣價賣給進口商。例如 100 支燈管破了 17 支，如果買方向賣方再次購買 17 支的話來補足 100 支，其中的 10 支可以算折扣價，另外 7 支則需要以原價計算。而且通常損壞的那些也不須再寄回去，這些都可以跟出口商談。

慣用語

1. under tight deadline 到期的時間很緊迫、快截止了

I got to hand this report in. It is **under tight deadlines**.

我要趕快把這份報告交進去，快要截止的。

---

2. proof of something 以資證明、提出某種證明

I need to provide **proof of** identify and address to renew my driver's license.

我需要提供身分證明還有戶籍地的證明文件才能換新的駕照。

Unit 25
商品品質不良，要求提供折扣

Janice 的公司向 Mr. Garcia 的公司進口一批高級魚排，可是到貨發現品質很差，所以 Janice 向 Mr. Garcia 提出退款折扣的要求。

 人物角色

- Mr. Garcia　　　國外出口商
- Janice　　　　　台灣進口商

信件內容

Dear Mr. Garcia,

Thanks for the delivery of our order PO. Number 228430 dated 3rd July 2017. The cargo has arrived and been unloaded a couple of days ago.

While we were unloading, we recorded 200 boxes of grade A salmon fillet, 35 boxes of cleaned squid tubes, and 46 boxes of ribbon fish which is the same as our order.

However, we are **in doubt** about the quality of the grade A salmon fillet. We thawed two boxes to inspect the quality. The size is very small and the freshness is not at its best. In addition, the color is **more on the pale side**, which is not red. We do not think this should be classified as grade A product. We will not be able to resale these salmon filets as premium product. Therefore, we are asking a 20% discount on the unit price for the salmon fillet to cover our loss. Please find the photos attached for your reference.

Await for your reply.

Thanks & regards,
Janice Chung

親愛的賈西亞先生，

我們前幾天已經收到我們 2017 年 7 月 3 號所下的 228430 號訂單的貨了，貨櫃也已經拆卸完成。

我們拆卸點貨的過程中，我們收了 200 箱的 A 級鮭魚排，35 箱的魷魚筒，還有 46 箱的白帶魚，數量與我們訂購的相符合。

可是我們對 A 級鮭魚排的品質很有疑慮，我們退冰了兩箱魚排來檢查品質，實際上的魚排小片，鮮度也不好，而且顏色也偏白，並不紅潤，我們覺得這個不是 A 級鮭魚排該有的品質。我們沒有辦法用高級貨的價格賣給我們的客戶。

因此，我們要求貴公司提供魚排單價減少 20%的折扣給我們來補償我們的損失，附上照片供您參考。

期待您的回覆。

謝謝，
珍妮絲・莊

王牌助理的小祕訣

　　對於生鮮食品的採購，爭議性會比較大，協商賠償的情況也容易發生，尤其是沒有可以信任的人員可以去做採購前檢測的情況下，只能相信出口商的片面之詞，還有照片之類的文件來支持出口商的講法。有的公司會聘僱檢測人員到當地去驗貨，但不是每間公司都有這種預算。所以跟有誠信的廠商購買是很重要的，有誠信的廠商也會比較願意談賠償的事宜。

 慣用語

1. in doubt 懷疑、有疑慮

Unless I saw it in writing; otherwise, I am **in doubt** about he would offer me a better deal.

除非是白紙黑字，不然我不太相信他會給我比較有利的條件。

---

2. more on the (adj.) side 比較偏（形容詞）怎麼樣

I think it is about right, but **more on the lighter side**.

我覺得差不多，可是好像偏輕了一點。

Unit 26
通知訂房紀錄，會議行程安排

Mr. Jenkins 將到台灣拜訪幾個客戶，他主要的行程是由台灣的代理商幫忙安排，台灣的助理將安排好的行表交代給 Mr. Jenkins 的助理。

人物角色

- Mr. Jenkins   國外訪客
- Natalie   Mr. Jenkins 的助理
- M. Huang   台灣代理商
- Teresa   Mr. Huang 的助理

信件內容

Dear Natalie,

Greetings, we have put together a visiting schedule for Mr. Jenkins regarding his upcoming visit in Sep. Please find the summary below:

25th Sep   Airport pick up for Mr. Jenkins at 8:45 pm

26th Sep   Meeting with Mr. Huang at 10 am (Hotel pick up at 9:30 am)
Lunch with Mr. Huang at 12 pm
Site visit and meeting with Sheng Yong company at 2:00 pm

27th Sep   Meeting with Da-Yi company at 11:00 am (Hotel pick up at 10 am)
Drop off Mr. Jenkins at high speed rail station at 3:00 pm

Mr. Jenkins is booked in to stay in the Grand palace hotel for the night of 25th and 26th Sep.

Mr. Huang would like to meet with Mr. Jenkins to ensure they are **on the same page** prior to their meeting with Sheng Yong company in the morning of the 26th. If there is any issue Mr. Jenkins would like to discuss, it will be a good time.

Thanks & regards,
Teresa Tsai

親愛的娜塔莉，

您好，我們幫金克斯先生安排了幾個他九月份將訪問的行程，行程如下：

9/25　8:45 pm 到機場接金克斯先生
9/26　10:00 am 與黃先生開會（9:30 飯店接送）
　　　12:00 pm 與黃先生共進午餐
　　　2:00 pm 與昇陽公司開會及廠房參觀
9/27　11:00 am 與達英公司開會（10:00 飯店接送）
　　　3:00 pm 送金克斯先生到高鐵站

25 號及 26 號晚上金克斯將會下榻皇宮酒店。

黃先生想在 26 號早上我們拜訪昇陽公司之前，先跟金克斯先生開會，互相了解一下目前的情況。如果金克斯先生有什麼議題想討論的，可以趁這個時間提出來。

謝謝，
泰瑞莎・蔡

王牌助理的小祕訣

　　在為國外廠商或客戶安排會議行程的時候，如果有需要與公司一起去拜訪終端客戶的情況，最好先與國外訪客開個會，先達成共識。有什麼議題可以談，客戶大概會問些什麼問題或是什麼議題需要避免與客戶討論。畢竟每家公司的經營方針還有策略不同，萬一訪客的說法與公司有出入，這會造成終端客戶對公司產生疑問。

慣用語

1. **drop off** 放下，載某人到某處

Can you **drop off** this parcel at the office for me, please?

你可以幫我把這包東西拿到公司放嗎？

---

2. **on the same page** 達到共識

Are we **on the same page** now? I don't want you to think I want to transfer to Taipei office.

我這樣講清楚嗎？我不想讓你認為我想調去台北分公司。

前情提要

Mr. Jenkins 看過 Teresa 傳來的會議行程表後,他交代 Natalie 跟對方說他想要討論的一些事項。

人物角色

- Mr. Jenkins　　　國外訪客
- Natalie　　　　　Mr. Jenkins 的助理
- M. Huang　　　　台灣代理商
- Teresa　　　　　Mr. Huang 的助理

信件內容

Dear Teresa,

　　Thanks for your e-mail regarding the meeting agenda. Mr. Jenkins would like to add a few things in his meeting with Mr. Huang.

First of all, he would like to discuss the progress of the renewable energy project. The primary design was completed and presented to the end user **a while ago**, and he would like to know the feedback from the end user.

Secondly, he would like to discuss the estimated sales figure for next year. The total sales of year 2016 dropped 10% compared with the sales figure of year 2015. He would like to know is there anything we can do to provide to assist you further, such as sales presentation and customer visits.

If you require any more brochures or leaflets, please feel free to let us know. We will be able to put together a package for you.

Thanks & regards,
Natalie Fisher

泰瑞莎您好，

　　謝謝您傳來的議程表，金克斯先生有幾件事想跟黃先生討論一下。

　　首先，他想討論再生能源的那個案子的進度，原始的設計已經在好一陣子前給客戶看過了，他想要知道客戶有沒有什麼意見。

　　第二項，他想要談一下明年的銷售業績預測。2016 年的業績比 2015 年下滑了大概一成，他想知道有沒有什麼我們可以做得更好的地方，例如商品簡報或是客戶拜訪之類的。

　　如果你有需要商品簡介或傳單，歡迎通知我們，我們會立即幫您準備。

　　謝謝，
　　娜塔莉・費雪

01
PART
國
貿
口
說
篇

02
PART
國
貿
寫
作
篇

王牌助理的小祕訣

　　如果有想討論的議題，不妨先通知對方，這樣對方也比較有時間去準備，訪客在會議中得到的資訊也會比較完整。如果等到見面時再提出來，那等到對方有機會得到答案時，訪客也早已離開，就失去面對面討論的便利性。因為很多助理也需要負責為老闆翻譯，所以盡早知道內容，助理們翻譯起來也比較順手。

慣用語

1. first of all 首先

First of all, we need to get everyone together and let them know the emergency drill plan.

首先，我們要先集合所有的人，然後再跟大家說明緊急情況演習的處理步驟。

2. a while ago 不久前

I met Nicolas **a while ago**, and he seems like a pretty nice guy.

我是不久之前認識尼可拉斯的，他人還挺不錯。

Unit 28
會議記錄

前情提要

國外的客戶到台灣來開會，對方的秘書要求台灣的聯絡窗口傳一份會議紀錄給她留底。

人物角色

- Nicole　　　　　　國外客戶的秘書
- Mr. Parson　　　　國外訪客
- Mr. Grainger　　　國外訪客
- C.M. Chou　　　　台灣公司的負責人
- Sheryl Wang　　　台灣公司的助理／秘書

信件內容

Dear Nicole,

As per your request, please find the meeting minutes below:

Type of Meeting: General visitors meeting
Date and time: 23rd May 2017 at 10:00 am
Facilitator: C.M. Chou
Attendees present: K. Parson & J. Grainger
Absent: None
Meeting agenda:
1. Customer complaint handling
2. Sales figure forecast for year 2017
3. Quality control issues

Reports:

Report given by C.M. Chou for an overview of general performance in year 2016.
Report given by C.M. Chou regarding customer complaint from Tao Yuan factory.

Open issues:

Unable to **reach an agreement with** Tao Yuan factory regarding the refund amount.

Action items:

J Grainger to visit Tao Yuan factory to execute the investigation and report to K. Parson to determine the payout.

C.M. Chou to persuade Tao Yuan factory not to return the shipment.

Please kindly ask Mr. Parson and Mr. Grainger to sign the minutes if there is nothing they wish to add or amend.

Thanks & regards,
Sheryl Wang

中譯

親愛的妮可，

如您所要求的，附上會議記錄一份。

會議種類：訪客會議

日期及時間：2017 年 5 月 23 日上午 10 點
會議主辦人：周建明
出席人員：克里斯帕森及強森安傑
缺席者：無
會議討論事項：
1. 客訴及處理
2. 2017 年的銷售業績預測
3. 品管的問題

進度報告：

由周建明報告 2016 年的整體表現
由周建明報告桃園廠的客訴問題。

待處理的問題：
仍無法與桃園廠達成賠償金額的協議。

需執行的事項：

強森安傑到桃園廠去執行調查並向克里斯帕森報告，由克里斯帕森決定賠償的金額。

由周建明去說服客戶不要退貨。

麻煩請帕森還有安傑先生確認一下會議紀錄的內容，如果不需更改，則請他們簽名確認。

謝謝，
雪若‧王

王牌助理的小祕訣

　　大部分的國外訪客到台灣訪問都不會帶著秘書出門，但是稱職的秘書一定需要了解老闆出門跟客戶談了什麼事。所以最好的方式就是跟對方要一份會議紀錄，上面會清楚記錄會議中決議的事項還有待處理的事項，因為通常秘書需要去追蹤及處理後續。老闆通常只會交代需要處理的事項，不會交代細節，所以有會議紀錄可以讓秘書或助理清楚了解為什麼老闆交辦這些事。

慣用語

1. **as per your request 依照您的要求**

As per your request, the sales reports for the past 6 months are here.

依照您的要求，過去六個月的業績報告都找出來了。

---

2. **reach an agreement with someone 與某人達成協議**

I **have reached an agreement with Rebecca**, and she will be working half day on Saturdays from now on.

我已經跟瑞貝卡談好了，所以現在開始她星期六都上半天。

Unit 29
會議待處理事項，處理進度報告

((📡)) 前情提要

　　國外廠商來訪時，為了處理客訴問題，親自拜訪的桃園廠並進行調查，現在調查結果出爐了，他們向台灣的廠商報告。

👤 人物角色

- Nicole Gibson　　國外客戶的秘書
- Mr. Parson　　　國外訪客
- Mr. Grainger　　國外訪客
- C.M. Chou　　　台灣公司的負責人
- Sheryl Wang　　台灣公司的助理／秘書

📧 信件內容

Dear Sheryl,

　　Thanks for your email, we would like to update you on the finding of the investigation, which **took place** last month on Mr. Grainger's visit to Tao

Yuan factory.

We have sent a sample of the batch that we supplied to Tao Yuan factory early January 2017 for testing. The result does not reflect any significant change in quality and durability. However, the formula and combination of the compound were modified to be more heat resistant. This still does not explain why Tao Yuan factory is having so many problems with this product.

If Tao Yuan factory insists on the return of the product, it will lose on cost of shipping. We would like Mr. Chou to discuss with them and offer them 10% discount **as a gesture of goodwill** to cover their inconvenience; however, please make it clear this is not a compensation for the faulty product.

Looking forward to hearing from you.

Kind regards,
Kris Parson

中譯

親愛的雪若,

　　謝謝您的來信,我們想通知您有關上個月安傑先生到桃園廠進行的調查報告結果。

　　我們送了 2017 年一月初出貨給桃園廠同一批的樣品去化驗,化驗結果並沒有顯示品質及耐受度有何不妥。但是生產配方和複合物的組合是有為了讓產品修正成更耐高溫。這還是無法解釋為什麼桃園廠使用上一直有問題。

　　如果桃園廠堅持要退貨的話,那他們會損失運費,我們希望周先生可以跟客戶談談,我們願意提供一成的折扣,但是請跟客戶特別強調這並不是承認我們的產品有問題,而是體諒他們使用上遇到這麼多麻煩。

　　期待您的回覆,

　　謝謝
　　克里斯帕森

王牌助理的小祕訣

　　客訴是常常會遇見的課題，尤其是生鮮食品類對於品質的認定的爭議性更大。解決的方式常常是基於互信的原則，除非是很大的問題，否則只要供應商稍做讓步，通常就能解決。如果是可以測試的產品，不妨提供測試報告給客戶，畢竟有時候出問題的不是商品本身，可能是使用者操作或者是保存上的問題，只是這點很難提出證明。

慣用語

1. take place 發生、舉行

The end of year banquet will **take place** at Hyatt hotel this year.

今年的尾牙會在凱悅飯店舉辦。

----

2. a gesture of goodwill 釋出善意

I bought him a coffee as **a gesture of goodwill**.

我請他喝咖啡算是跟他和好了。

Unit 30
工程師、訪客的邀請函及簽證問題

前情提要

　　Daisy 是 Cassandra 公司的台灣代理商，因為工程師要申請工作簽證的關係，Daisy 提前準備了工程師需要的邀請函給 Cassandra。

人物角色

- Cassandra　　　國外聯繫窗口
- Daisy　　　　　台灣代理商

信件內容

Dear Cassandra,

　　Please find the invitation for the engineers below, Alex needs to take this with him to the Taiwanese embassy when he **launches the working visa application** for himself.

To who it may concern

Re: Work permit application for Mr. Alex Hoffmann

On behalf of New River Company, I would like to invite Mr. Alex Hoffmann to Taiwan to execute installation for feeding system in Tai Hsin steel company for the duration of 3 months. Mr. Hoffmann is scheduled to arrive in Taiwan on the 9th Aug 2017 and stays until 9th Nov 2017. Please kindly **grant the work permit** for Mr. Alex Hoffmann accordingly.

Please find Mr. Alex Hoffmann's detail below:
Full name: Alex Finn Hoffmann
Date of birth: 3rd May 1973
Passport number: F10993881
Country of issue: Germany

Should you require any additional information, please feel free to contact me on: +886 52250098

Yours truly,
Daisy Lee

親愛的卡珊卓，

　　隨信附上工程師的邀請函，艾力克斯霍夫曼先生要申請工作簽證時需要帶邀請函到台灣的大使館。

　　致相關人士

　　代表新河公司，我們需要邀請請艾利可斯霍夫曼先生到台灣的泰鑫鋼鐵公司執行送料系統的安裝工作。期間約需要三個月，艾力克斯霍夫曼先生預計在 2017 年 8 月 9 日抵達台灣，預計停留到 11 月 9 日。麻煩請核發需要的工作簽證給他。艾力克斯霍夫曼先生的資料如下：

　　全名：艾力克斯‧芬恩‧霍夫曼
　　生日：1973 年 5 月 3 日
　　護照號碼：F10993881
　　發照國家：德國

　　如果需要其他補充資料的話，麻煩請聯絡我，電話是：
+886 52250098

　　謝謝，
　　黛絲‧李

王牌助理的小祕訣

　　如果需要國外工程師到台灣執行安裝或維修工作時，記得要提醒對方到當地的台灣駐外代表處或大使館申請工作簽證。申請簽證時需要附上台灣公司所發的工作邀請函，邀請函上需要註明工程師的明細，例如生日及護照號碼等等。邀請函上也需要註明停留的長度，駐外單位可能會要求工程師提供機票的訂位證明，再依據邀請函上的日期發簽證。

慣用語

1. launch the application 提出申請

When is the last day to **launch the application**?

最晚在哪一天要提出申請？

---

2. grant the visa / permit 核發簽證／許可證

These are the documents that you need for them to **grant you the landing visa.**

你需要提供這些文件他們才會核發落地簽證給你。

Unit 31
確認是否還在保固期內

((·)) 前情提要

　　工程師在台灣進行安裝工作的時候，客戶跟他反應另外一台機器上的定位裝置有問題，請他看看是不是可以調整一下。

人物角色

- Michael　　　　原廠工程師統籌人員
- Sean　　　　　工程師
- Brenda　　　　台灣代理商

信件內容

Dear Michael,

　　The installation for the packaging line is going as scheduled. However, the factory reflected a problem with the print mark registration device in machine number K89342. The sensor seems to be faulty which is unable to detect the correct cutting

01
PART
國
貿
口
說
篇

02
PART
國
貿
寫
作
篇

position.

According to our record, this print mark registration was only purchased and installed last year. We believe it is still under warranty. Sean attempted to adjust the sensor setting; however, it did not solve the problem. He believed that the sensor system needed to be replaced completely.

Please **verify against** your record and kindly organize a replacement sensor to be delivered as soon as possible. The factory is hoping they can **take the advantage of** Sean being here and have him replace the sensor for them. Please kindly confirm whether it is possible.

Looking forward to hearing from you.

Best regard,
Brenda Wu

麥克您好，

　　生產線的安裝工作很順利，可是工廠反應另一台機台，機台號碼 K89342 的定位裝置有問題，上面的感應器好像有問題，沒有辦法偵測正確的裁切位置。

　　我們查過購買紀錄，這組定位裝置是去年才安裝的，我們相信還在保固期內。西恩有試著去調整感應器的設定，可是沒有用，他也覺得感應器需要整組更換。

　　麻煩您對照一下你的紀錄，請盡快將新的感應器寄來。工廠希望能趁著西恩還在的時候請他更換，麻煩您確認是不是可以這樣安排。

　　期待您的回覆。

　　謝謝
　　布蘭達・吳

王牌助理的小祕訣

　　客戶通常是很聰明的，尤其是當有國外工程師來駐廠執行安裝或是維修工作的時候，客戶會盡量利用工程師的時間，請他們幫忙解決其他機器的問題。可是因為合約及費用上的問題，通常可以幫的小忙，工程師會盡量。可是如果需要修理或更換大項目，工程師必須向公司知會，公司同意的話他們才會去執行，畢竟安裝及維修也是當一項商品在賣。

慣用語

1. verify against 查證，對照

My memory is not so reliable; I need to **verify against** the paperwork.

我的記憶力不太靠得住，我需要查證一下紙本資料。

----

2. take the advantage of 趁這個機會，佔便宜

I am going to **take the advantage of** the cheap airfare and book myself a holiday.

我要趁機票便宜的時候去渡個假。

Unit 32
安裝時發現零件短缺

工程師在跟客戶一起開箱的時候發覺好像少了東西，代理商趕緊向原廠確認是不是有缺少。

 人物角色

- Stephen　　　國外原廠聯絡窗口
- Hannah　　　代理商

✉ 信件內容

Dear Stephen,

Hope you are well. Patrick **went through** the parts for the installation today. He suspects one of the cables for the interface control panel was not packed in the parts box. According to the packing list, the interface control panel and the cable should be in the same carton. However, the cable

01
PART

國
貿
口
說
篇

02
PART

國
貿
寫
作
篇

is not in it. **FYI**, the part number for the cable is HG6672.

Would you be able to check your shipment coordinator for our order please to see If the cable was packed in a separated carton. If so, then we would be able to locate it eventually. However, if the cable did not come with the shipment, please kindly arrange one to be couriered to us ASAP.

The factory has completed the process of offloading the cargo, and the positioning will commence in two days. We are hoping the cable would arrive by the end of the week.

Thanks & regards,
Hannah Yang

親愛的史蒂芬，

　　您好，派崔克今天看過了要安裝的零件了，他覺得好像少了一條人機介面控制板的連接線。我們查過包裝單，人機介面控制板跟連接線應該要在同一個箱子裡，可是我們沒有找到。讓您知道一下，那一條連接線的型號是 HG6672。

　　可以請你跟你的出貨人員查一下嗎？看看那條連接線是不是裝到別的箱子去了，如果有的話，那我們一定找的到。如果漏掉的話，那就請您趕快補寄一條給我們。

　　工廠昨天已經把所有的貨櫃下完了，兩天之後就要開始定位了，希望連接線可以在周末之前寄到。

　　謝謝，
　　漢娜‧楊

王牌助理的小祕訣

　　零件開箱的時候,如果有工程師在場,他們通常會檢查一下零件有沒有到齊。經驗老到的工程師常常一眼就會發現是不是有少了零件,如果找不到的話,會先對一下包裝單,看看零件是否有列在包裝單上。如果沒有列在包裝單上,很可能是出貨時漏掉了。有時候可能是包裝貨物的管理人員把零件裝到別的箱子裡。可以先跟國外供應商聯絡請他們查一下。

慣用語

1. go through 經歷過,用掉,涵蓋,尋找

I **went through** everything, but I still couldn't find the report.

我該找的都找了,可是還是找不到那份報告。

-----

2. FYI (for your information) 供您參考,讓您知道一下

FYI, Tommy will attend the meeting on Joe's behalf tomorrow.

先通知您一下,明天湯米會代表喬伊去參加明天的會議。

Unit 33
討論安裝進度

Peter 通知 Jennifer 工程師們要一月份才會有空到台灣進行安裝工作，可是這樣會遇到農曆新年的假期，Jennifer 希望 Peter 能夠安排工程師 12 月就到台灣。

人物角色

- Peter　　　　　　總公司工程師統籌人員
- Jennifer　　　　　代理商／台灣分公司代表

信件內容

Dear Peter,

　　Thanks for your email, I understand engineers are scheduled to complete their installation in India before they can **move on** to the projects in Taiwan. Because the factory will be closed for 9 days during Chinese New Year. The engineers would waste at least a week here. Therefore, they would have to be in Taiwan for at least 10 and half weeks.

The client also wishes to have this project completed before the new year, so we believe that **it makes more sense** if the engineers can start two weeks early, which is on 25th Dec if possible.

Please let us know whether this would line up with their schedule. If it works for you, then please arrange the engineers to arrive on either the 23rd or the 24th Dec. We will make the necessary regarding the accommodation and transportation.

Kind regards,
Jennifer Lee

親愛的彼得,

　　謝謝你的來信。我了解工程師要先完成印度的安裝工作才能到台灣。因為工廠在農曆新年的時候會休九天假。工程師會浪費至少一個星期。所以他們至少要在台灣待上十個半星期。

　　客戶希望這個案子可以在年底前結案,我們覺得如果可以提早兩個星期,在 12 月 25 號開工的話,會最適當。

　　麻煩您確認這樣有沒有辦法配合上工程師的行程,如果你可以接受的話,那請安排工程師在 23 或 24 號抵達台灣。我們會安排住宿還有交通相關的事項。

　　謝謝,
　　珍妮佛‧李

王牌助理的小祕訣

　　有時候因為合約或是客戶要求的關係，代理商需要與總公司搶工程師用，如果工程師的行程很滿，無法配合台灣的客戶要求，那可以請總公司看看是否可以調其他的工程師來執行。有時候同一個案子卻需要動用到兩組不同的工程師來執行，一組做開頭，另外一組做結尾。這是大家都不樂見的結果可是也沒辦法，唯有這樣才能順利完工。

慣用語

1. **move on** 接下一個、繼續下一個

I think we have covered everything in this topic, and we can **move on** to the next.

這個主題已經涵蓋的差不多了，所以我們可以談下一個主題了。

----

2. **make sense** 合理、有道理

I don't believe what he just said because it **makes no sense**.

我不相信他剛剛說的話，因為完全不合理。

Unit 34
安裝進度報告

前情提要

Annie 向 Hector 報告目前在台灣工程安裝的進度。

人物角色

- Annie   台灣分公司／代理商
- Hector   國外總公司聯絡窗口

信件內容

Dear Hector,

The installation for the Tai-Chung project is **going well**. The positioning is done and the engineers are working on the linking of different components. The primary linking will be completed by end of the week, and once the electrician connects the main power supply, the machine should able to function by mid next week.

According to the schedule, the engineers will be spending 4 weeks working on linking and adjusting the production line. If all goes well, we will be able to do the test run on week 5, which is the week beginning on 4th Aug.

We have ordered the testing material for this project, expecting it to arrive in the factory early July. The engineers should have enough material to test the machine before the final acceptance run.

Hopefully, it will go as planned. I will notify you immediately if there is any change or delay.

Thanks & regards,
Annie Kuo

赫特您好，

目前在台中安裝的案子進行的順利，機械的定位已完成，工程師正在著手不同部分的連接。這個星期五前就可以完成初階的連接。等電工把電源接上之後，機械下個星期裡就可以啟動了。

就如原本預定的行程，連接及調整機器大概需要四星期，如果順利的話，我們應該在第五周可以開始驗收，也就是 8 月 4 日的那個禮拜。

測試材料也已經訂好了，預計七月初就可以就會到工廠，一直到最後測試驗收前，工程師應該有足夠的材料來調整機器。

希望一切都可以順利進行，如果有延誤或更改的話我們會立即通知您。

謝謝，
安妮·郭

王牌助理的小祕訣

　　代理商或是分公司的角色就是國外總公司在台灣的眼睛，跟總公司保持密切的聯繫是工作的一部分，尤其是總公司的工程師在台灣執行安裝或維修工作的時候。雖然總公司了解安裝或維修所需要的時間長度，但他們也需要掌握過程是否順利，是否有其他問題產生。工程師也通常還有其他工作在等著他們去執行，所以總公司需要掌握他們能否準時地完成指派的工作。

 慣用語

1. going well 很順利

Things are **going** very **well** between Charlie and Lina; I can hear the wedding bells.

查理和麗娜進展得很順利，我相信他們應該很快就會結婚了。

2. according to 依照

According to the latest news, Jeff will be promoted to be the manager.

我聽到最新的消息說，傑夫會是下一任的經理。

Unit 35
耽誤到工程師的行程

Justine 是 Tyler 公司的台灣代理商，目前有工程師在台灣安裝機器，可是因為測試材料的問題，Justine 想跟 Tyler 先提醒一下工程師可能會耽誤到工程師回去的時間。

人物角色

- Tyler　　　　　工程師統籌人員
- Justine　　　　國內代理商

信件內容

Dear Tyler,

　　Just to **give you a heads up** regarding the possible delay regarding the installation project here. We are having problems to source the suitable material for the test run.

As you are aware, this new production line is designed to produce a new brand, which has a different dimension than the rest. There is no existing material that we can use, and everything has to be custom-made for this design. It is not only costly but also time-consuming. We located one supplier who is willing to manufacture the testing materials for us; however, his best delivery is 3 weeks from now.

We are hoping that this would not cause too much delay since we've still got approximately 2 weeks before the test run. However, please be prepared that the engineers might have to **stay back** for extra week.

We will keep you updated with any progress.

Thanks & regards,
Justine Chang

親愛的泰勒，

　　我想先跟您説一聲，目前這個安裝的案子可能會有延誤。要找到適當的測試材料有點困難。

　　您大概也了解，這條新的生產線是設計來生產新的品牌，所以產品的尺寸也跟其他的品牌不同。目前沒有現成的材料可以測試，全部需要訂做。除了價格很高之外，交貨期也是個大問題。我們找到一個廠商願意幫我們生產，可是他的交貨期從今天算起還需要三星期。

　　我們希望這個延誤不會造成太大的麻煩，因為我們大概還有兩個星期才會做測試，可是希望你有心理準備，工程師們大概需要多待一個星期。

　　如果有其他後續的發展我們會持續跟你保持聯絡。

　　謝謝，
　　賈絲汀・張

王牌助理的小祕訣

　　一旦發現將會延誤到工程師的時間，一定要盡早知會國外原廠。因為很多時候工程師的安裝工作是一個接著一個，時間很緊湊。其實可以先問一下工程師，因為他們大概都知道工作銜接的其間有多少空檔，如果不是直接要接下一個工作的話，那耽誤到的就只是他們私人休息的時間。除此之外，記得要確認他們的工作簽證，如果還要延簽，那就很麻煩。

慣用語

1. give someone a heads up 提醒、讓某人有心理準備、預先通知某人

I just want to **give you a heads up** before Johnson calls you in.

在強森叫你進去之前，我只想先讓你有個心理準備

----

2. stay back 留下來、待命

Marshal is going to **stay back** to provide technical support.

馬歇爾會留下來做技術支援。

Unit 36
公司內部職務調動通知

前情提要

　　Linda 原本是負責國外文書的助理，現在要調到業務部做業務，她寫信通知國外的聯絡人職務變動的事情。

人物角色

- Donna　　　　　國外廠商聯絡人
- Linda　　　　　國內公司助理

信件內容

Dear Donna,

　　I am pleased to notify you that I have gotten an internal promotion to be transferred to Sales Department to be a sales consultant. The promotion will **come into effect** on 5th of May 2017 which is three weeks from now. Sadly, I will be leaving my current role as the administration assistant on 30th April 2017. I would like to **take this opportunity to** express my appreciation for your assistance during my role as the administration assistant.

Please allow me to introduce Miss. Katrina Lin, she will be taking over the role as the administration assistant from 1st of May 2017. She is very experienced in international trading practice, and I believe she will be able to provide the same service to you continuously. Please use the same extension to contact Miss. Lin. My email address will remain unchanged. Please keep in touch, and I would love to hear from you in the future.

Yours truly,
Linda Huang

唐娜您好，

　　有個好消息跟您分享，我很榮幸的要調職到業務部當業務人員，人事命令將在 2017 年五月五日生效，也就是三個禮拜之後。很難過的是，我即將在四月三十日離開目前這個文書助理的職位，我想藉這個機會向您道謝，在我任職文書助理的這段時間您對我的照顧。

　　讓我向您介紹卡崔娜・林，她即將在 2017 年五月一日接手文書助理的工作，她對國際貿易的業務很熟悉，相信她一定可以駕輕就熟。以後請還是用我這個分機號碼來連絡她。我的電子郵件信箱沒有變，希望我們未來還是能保持聯絡。

　　謝謝，
　　琳達・黃

01
PART
國
貿
口
說
篇

02
PART
國
貿
寫
作
篇

 王牌助理的小祕訣

　　無論是公司內部的職務調動或是因為其他個人因素要離職，向原本負責的客戶打聲招呼是基本的禮貌，同時可以藉這個機會向國外的聯絡人致謝，畢竟大家可能合作已有一段時間了，其中有很多受到對方照顧的機會，商業關係也可以昇華成友誼。如果本身有意願，而公司也不反對的話，也可以把自己私人的電子郵件地址或電話給對方留底。

 慣用語

1. **come into effect** 生效

The new tax law will **come into effect** next month.

新的稅制從下個月開始生效。

----

2. **take the opportunity to** 藉這個機會、順水推舟

Robin decides to **take the opportunity to** discuss his concern with Nick about doing overtime constantly

羅賓剛好藉著這個機會好好跟尼克談談經常加班的問題。

篇章回顧

✅ 精選常用慣用語

1. **address to** 寫給某人

This letter is **addressed to** the Finance Department.
Just pass it to Linda.

這封信是寄給財務部的，交給琳達就可以。

---

2. **pull out** 調出來

I have to **pull out** all the sales records from last month
to do the sales report.

我要把上個月的銷售紀錄都調出來才可以做銷售報告。

---

3. **got someone on the phone** 剛好某人打電話來

While you **got him on the phone**, can you check with
him whether there are more orders from today?

趁他還在線上，你趕快跟他確認看今天早上的訂單是否都給我
了嗎？

---

4. **other than** 除了

What else did you do **other than** staying at home on

the weekend?

你周末除了待在家之外還做了什麼？

---

5. **have something handy** 把某物準備好

Make sure you **have all the client contact details handy,** in case there is an emergency.

記得要把客戶的聯絡資料準備好，有急事的時候會用得上。

---

6. **check with someone** 詢問某人的意見

I need to <u>**check with**</u> Tony to see if he can attend the meeting on my behalf.

我需要問一下東尼看他是不是可以代表我去開會。

---

7. **get back to someone** 回覆給某人

Don't forget to **get back to** Jessica. She is still waiting for an answer.

別忘了潔西卡還在等你的回覆。

---

8. **go through** 對照、再檢查一次

Can we **go through** the speech again please? I am worried about I would make mistakes.

我們可以再對照一次講稿的內容嗎？我怕我會出錯。

---

9. **double check** 再次確認

I am not sure about our refund policy; you might want to

double check with the manager.

我不太清楚我們的退貨條件，你可能要再跟經理確認一下。

---

10. **just to be on the safe side** 這樣比較保險

Maybe we should schedule extra staff for the weekend rush **just to be on the safe side**.

我們不如多安排一點人手來應付周末的人潮，這樣比較保險。

---

11. **got off the phone with someone** 跟某人講完電話

I just **got off the phone with** my boss. He wants me to follow up with the textile case.

我剛跟我老闆講完電話，他交代我要追蹤一下紡織廠的那個案子。

---

12. **upgrade to** 升級、更換

I want to **upgrade** my car **to** an automatic.

我想把我的車換成自排的。

---

13. **compatible with** 可相容的、可以配合使用

The iphone headphone is not **compatible with** Android system.

Iphone 的耳機與安卓系統不相容

---

14. **someone had better** 某人…最好…

You'd better finish this report before lunch time. I think

Jim needs it for the meeting at 3.

你最好在中午前把這份報告打好，吉姆三點開會的時候可能要用到。

---

15. **The thing is... 可是，是這樣的…**

The thing is. I don't want to tell him because I don't know how he feels about me.

是這樣的，因為我不知道他是怎麼看待我的，所以我不想跟他提。

---

16. **A bit of delay 延遲，出狀況**

I am afraid you won't be able to pick up your car today. There is **a bit of delay** and the car is not ready.

很抱歉你今天可能沒有辦法把車牽回去，因為有點狀況，你的車還沒弄好。

---

17. **the same as something 與某物相同**

His phone is **the same as** mine.

他的手機跟我的一樣。

---

18. **work on something 處理中、正在安排**

I have been **working on** this project since 3 months ago.

我三個月前開始負責這個專案。

---

19. consolidate into 集中、合併

I got three orders ready for Amanda. I will **consolidate into** single shipment for her.

我有三個亞曼達的訂單都好了，我會幫她併貨一起出。

---

20. in that case 這樣的話

In that case, I think I will go in to work early tomorrow morning.

如果是這樣的話，那我明天一早一點到公司好了。

---

21. be entitled to 有資格

You are **entitled to** annual bonus once you stayed a full year in this company.

如果你在公司待滿一年後，你有就資格可以領年終。

---

22. put something / someone on hold 暫停、稍等

Sorry I can **put you on hold** for a minute please, I am on another line.

可以麻煩請你稍等嗎？我現在還在接另一通電話。

---

23. first thing tomorrow 明早立即處理

I promise the report will be ready for you **first thing tomorrow**.

我保證那份報表明天你進公司就會在你桌上。

---

24. **on to it** 處理、進行中

I know this invoice needs to be fixed. I am **on to it**.

我知道這份對帳單要重做,我會處理。

---

25. **sure thing** 當然、一定

Sure thing! I can help you with entertaining the visitors.

當然,我可以幫你招待客戶。

---

26. **have a word with someone** 與某人談一談

I don't know what I have done. The manager wants to **have a word with** me.

我不知道我到底做了什麼。經理說要找我談一談。

---

27. **take a message** 留言

If anyone called for me, can you **take a message** please?

如果有人打電話給我,可以麻煩你幫我留言嗎?

---

28. **put in a request** 申請,要求

I just realised Tommy **put in a request** to be transferred to Sales.

我剛聽說湯米要申請調到銷售部。

---

29. **upon receipt of payment** 收到款項之後

Your order will be shipped **upon receipt of payment**.

收到錢之後我們會馬上幫你出貨。

30. if it's not too much to ask 如果不是太麻煩的話

If it's not too much to ask, it will be great if you can take over my shift on Saturday.

如果不是太麻煩你的話，星期六可以跟你調班的話那就太棒了！

31. come out with something 想出、構想、整理出來

I need to come out with some fresh ideas to impress my boss.

我需要想一些比較有新意的構想，這樣才能打動我的老闆。

32. it is someone's call 只有某人可以決定

I really want to help you, but you know it is not my call.

我真的很想幫你，可是這不是我可以決定的。

33. put in a few good words 說幾句好話、求情

I want that promotion so bad. Do you think you can put in a few good words for me?

我好想要那個職位，你可以幫我美言幾句嗎？

34. courtesy call 好意的電話提醒

I got a courtesy call from my credit card company to say they haven't received the payment.

我接到信用卡公司打來的電話說我尚未付款。

35. **forward something to someone** 把某物交給某人

I got these documents for Jonny. Can you **forward them to him** please?

這些文件是要給強尼的，麻煩你轉交給他。

---

36. **ready to go** 準備好了

The projector is **ready to go**. We can have the meeting anytime.

投影機弄好了，隨時可以開會。

---

37. **make an amendment** 做修改

You'd better **make an amendment** on the invitation. You spelled Gary's last name wrong.

你最好把邀請函改一下，你把蓋瑞的姓拼錯了

---

38. **be liable for** 必須負擔

You **are liable for** all the damages if you don't have any insurance.

如果你沒有保險的話，出意外的時候你要負擔全部的賠償責任。

---

39. **up and running** 修好、準備好、可以用

I need to get this fax machine **up and running** ASAP. We are expecting an important document.

我需要叫人盡快把傳真機修好，我們在等一封重要的文件。

---

40. **ready to be picked up** 可以出貨了、好了

The consignment will be **ready to be picked up** in two days.

委託貨物再過兩天就可以出貨了。

---

41. **see what someone can do** 再看看能怎麼處理

I can't guarantee you that I can help you, but I will **see what I can do**.

我不能保證一定能幫你，可是我會盡量。

---

42. **one out of ten** 十個中有一個、十分之一（可用不同數量）

I bought a bag of apples from the supermarket yesterday, but 2 out of 5 are rotten.

我昨天到超市買了一包蘋果，可是五個裡面有兩顆是爛掉的。

---

43. **book someone in** 幫某人預約

Can you **book me in** for 10 o'clock tomorrow morning please?

你可以幫我約明天早上十點嗎？

---

44. **meeting minutes** 會議記錄

Who is taking the **meeting minutes** today?

今天的會議是輪到誰做紀錄？

---

45. **in the process of** 正在處理、在某過程中

She is **in the process of** getting a divorce. I don't think she is in a good mood.

她正在處理離婚的手續,所以心情應該不太好。

46. **put something through** 接通、下單

Can you **put the phone call through** to Nancy please? Her dad is on the phone.

可以叫南西來聽電話嗎?她爸爸打來。

47. **a small hiccup** 小問題

There is **a small hiccup**; otherwise, it would have been finished yesterday.

突然有點小問題,不然昨天就可以完工了。

48. **in advance** 提前

Can you notify me **in advance** for any meeting bookings, please? Otherwise, I won't be available.

如果要開會的話請提前通知我,不然我沒辦法出席。

49. **to be advised** 等候通知

Mr. Abbott has booked his flight, but where he would be staying is still **to be advised**.

亞伯特先生的航班訂好了,可是住哪裡還不知道。

50. when it comes to something 當談、說到到某事的時候

I always need Jerry's help **when it comes to** translation.

每次要翻譯東西的時候我就需要傑瑞來幫忙。

----

51. from something / sometime onwards 從某事／某時開始

The list price for all items will increase by 3% **from the next quarter onwards**.

從下一季開始所有品的牌價都將漲 **3%**。

----

52. take this opportunity to 趁這個機會

I would like to **take this opportunity to** thank Vanessa for her effort in this project.

我想趁這個機會謝謝凡妮莎對這的案子付出的心血。

----

53. meant to 應該要，註定的

I don't think we **meant to** take the right turn in the last intersection.

我覺得我們剛剛那個路口不應該右轉的。

----

54. every fortnight 每兩個禮拜，14 天

Sales report is due **every fortnight**.

每兩個禮拜我都要交銷售報告。

----

55. deduct from 扣除

The monthly insurance premium is **deducted from** my account automatically.

我的保險月費會自動從我的帳戶扣款。

56. the option of 選擇

He offered me **the option of** paying an installment because it would help my finance situation.

他說我可以分期付款，我覺得這樣對我的財務狀況來說比較適合。

57. line up 配合、銜接的上、等著

Ronald is trying to arrange a meeting with me, but our schedule just doesn't **line up**.

雷諾一直想跟我約見面，可是我們的行程怎麼樣都配合不了。

58. come off 卸下、掉下來

I was really embarrassed when the top button **came off** my shirt.

我襯衫最上面的那顆扣子突然掉下來，真是讓我丟臉死了。

59. put together 總裝、整合

We **put together** a small gift set for Jenny to congratulate her on her promotion.

我們大家選了幾項小禮物給珍妮來恭喜她升職了。

---

60. what steps to take 該怎麼處理、該怎麼做

I am not sure **what steps to take** in a situation like this.

這種情況我真的不知道跟如何處理。

---

61. under tight deadline 到期的時間很緊迫、快截止了

I got to hand this report in because it is **under a tight deadline**.

我要趕快把這份報告交進去，快要截止的。

---

62. proof of something 以資證明、提出某種證明

I need to provide **proof of** identify and address to renew my driver's license.

我需要提供身分證明還有戶籍地的證明文件才能換新的駕照。

---

63. launch the application 提出申請

When is the last day to **launch the application**?

最晚在哪一天要提出申請？

---

64. grant the visa / permit 核發簽證／許可證

These are the documents that you need for them to **grant you the landing visa**.

你需要提供這些文件他們才會核發落地簽證給你。

---

65. going well 很順利

Things are **going** very **well** between Charlie and Lina; I can hear the wedding bells.

查理和麗娜進展得很順利,我相信他們應該很快就會結婚了。

---

66. give someone a heads up 提醒、讓某人有心理準備、預先通知某人

I just want to **give you a heads up** before Johnson calls you in.

在強森叫你進去之前,我只想先讓你有個心理準備

---

67. stay back 留下來、待命

Marshal is going to **stay back** to provide technical support.

馬歇爾會留下來做技術支援。

---

68. come into effect 生效

The new tax law will **come into effect** next month.

新的稅制從下個月開始生效。

---

69. take the opportunity to 藉這個機會、順水推舟

Robin decides to **take the opportunity to** discuss his concern with Nick about doing overtime constantly

羅賓剛好藉著這個機會好好跟尼克談談經常加班的問題。

－考用・文法－

專為新多益綠、藍色證書為目標考生設計的 NEW TOEIC勝經!本書的文法整理淺顯易懂, 搭配重點題型詳解,讓考生立即掌握主題關鍵字與解題技巧,輕鬆拿高分!

書 系:Leader 010
書 名:新多益進分大絕招[文法]+[單字]
定 價:NT$ 380元
ISBN:978-986-90759-9-2
規 格:平裝/360頁/17x23cm/雙色印刷

有MP3的文法書!各類考試都適用! 讓考生們邊讀邊聽,在加強文法概念及擴充字彙同時強化寫作能力!

書 系:Learn Smart 043
書 名:iBT＋IELTS＋GMAT文法狀元的獨家私藏筆記
定 價:NT$ 380元
ISBN:978-986-90883-6-7
規 格:平裝/288頁/17x23cm/雙色印刷

跳脫英文文法「只看解析和例句」的學習框架, 讓電影台詞、文學名著、流行歌曲等經典名句帶領你在喜怒哀樂的情境中,學會英文文法!

書 系:Learn Smart 045
書 名:那些年我們一起熟悉的英文文法,藏在電影、小說、歌詞裡
定 價:NT$ 329元
ISBN:978-986-90883-8-1
規 格:平裝/336頁/17x23cm/雙色印刷

只要靈活運用在Instagram中出現的簡單英語句型PO文,就能寫出一篇好文章、輕鬆在各類英文寫作考試得高分!

書 系:Learn Smart 048
書 名:每日一句的Instagram PO文,輕鬆學好英文寫作
定 價:NT$ 349元
ISBN:978-986-91915-1-7
規 格:平裝/296頁/17x23cm/雙色印刷

－生活英語－

用故事區分，以及介系詞的"功能概念"分類，搭配圖解例句，考試不再和關鍵分數擦身而過，也是閱讀、寫作與口說的必備用書！

書　系：Leader 048
書　名：圖解介系詞、看故事學片語：第一本文法魔法書
定　價：NT$ 360元
ISBN：978-986-92856-7-4
規　格：平裝/320頁/17x23cm/雙色印刷

獨家吵架英語秘笈大公開！精選日常生活情境＋道地慣用語，教你適時地表達看法爭取應得的權利，成為最有文化的英語吵架王！

書　系：Learn Smart 064
書　名：冤家英語 (MP3)
定　價：NT$ 360元
ISBN：978-986-92855-6-8
規　格：平裝/304頁/17x23cm/雙色印刷/附光碟

享受異國風光，走訪知名美食熱點；帶著情感品嚐美食，才是人間美味；用英語表達富情感意涵的美食，才算得上是『食尚』。

書　系：Leader 050
書　名：餐飲英語：異國美食情緣(MP3)
定　價：NT$ 369元
ISBN：978-986-92856-9-8
規　格：平裝/288頁/17x23cm/雙色印刷/附光碟

職場英語系列 001

國貿人在全世界做生意的必備關鍵口說+Email（附 MP3）

作　　　者	陳幸美
發 行 人	周瑞德
執行總監	齊心瑀
行銷經理	楊景輝
企劃編輯	陳韋佑
封面構成	高鍾琪

內頁構成	菩薩蠻數位文化有限公司
印　　製	大亞彩色印刷製版股份有限公司
初　　版	2017 年 7 月
定　　價	新台幣 379 元
出　　版	倍斯特出版事業有限公司
電　　話	(02) 2351-2007
傳　　真	(02) 2351-0887
地　　址	100 台北市中正區福州街 1 號 10 樓之 2
E - m a i l	best.books.service@gmail.com
網　　址	www.bestbookstw.com

港澳地區總經銷	泛華發行代理有限公司
地　　址	香港新界將軍澳工業邨駿昌街 7 號 2 樓
電　　話	(852) 2798-2323
傳　　真	(852) 2796-5471

國家圖書館出版品預行編目資料

國貿人在全世界做生意的必備關鍵口說
+Email / 陳幸美著. -- 初版. -- 臺北
市：倍斯特, 2017.07面；　公分. --
（職業英語系列　；1）ISBN
978-986-94428-7-9(平裝附光碟片)
　1.商業英文 2.讀本

　805.18　　　　106009356